Allies of the
Storm

4393-LYNN

Allies of the Storm

Alan Lynn

4393-LYNN

This is a work of fiction. Names, characters, places and incidents either are the product of the author's imagination or are used fictitiously, and any resemblance to any actual persons, living or dead, events, or locales is entirely coincidental.

This book was printed in the United States of America.

To order additional copies of this book, contact:
Xlibris Corporation
1-888-7-XLIBRIS
www.Xlibris.com
Orders@Xlibris.com

Contents

TO … KYM

16 October, 1989—09:00

The Pentagon

Commander John Llewellyn sat patiently waiting for a meeting with his superior and very good friend Admiral Charles Benson, "Charlie" to those who knew him well. John and Charlie knew each other very well. That is why John had been asked to meet with Charlie this morning after picking up his retirement paperwork and hanging up his Navy blues for good old American civvies. At any moment, John knew he would be summoned into the Admiral's inner office. Charlie would be polluting the room with one of his obnoxious cigars and grinning from ear to ear like the proverbial cat who ate the canary. After all, today was to be a day when they could talk as friends and not a day of "business as usual." It was also the last time John would have to report to his superior; and, for the first time in John's military career, this fact brought with it feelings of both excitement and a sadness that only a fellow officer could truly understand.

God, John hated this office. Its overstuffed leather sofas smelled not at all of leather, but more like old cigars and an overbearing stench of sweat from so many officers who sat here waiting for orders they knew might take them to places from where they might never return. Not to mention the wall-to-wall bookcases filled with books no one cared about any more, let alone read. The dark paneled walls presented an even more foreboding atmosphere, but then again the Pentagon was never a place for social gatherings or light-hearted conversations.

John had been in this office on more than one occasion. Each time he was invited he was rewarded with new orders. Some he requested and some he wished to God he'd never seen. He'd been in all the trouble spots; Vietnam, Panama, Nicaragua . . . Brooklyn.! He also had all the medals to go along with it. He was most proud of the little "Good Conduct" medal. As an enlisted man, he had received it for 4 years of "undetected crime" before he was commissioned. He'd trade his Combat Actions, Navy Commendations, and Purple Hearts for the Good Conduct any day of the week. All the 'biggie' medals were for "being in the wrong place at the wrong time." When the 'troops' saw he had the Good Conduct Medal, they knew he had been "one of them" and there was an immediate respect and a bond that no academy grad would ever know.

At 38, John had been in the service for 20 years. He had joined the Navy in 1969, right out of high school, in order to avoid the draft. As he often put it, " I hated to walk so the Army was out, and the Marines got shot at too much so they were out. Now the Air Force had great creature comforts but the Navy had the best schools. The Air Force had this book that told you what you were allowed to do and the Navy had a book that told you what you were NOT allowed to do. So, I chose the Navy, that way I could do ANYTHING I wanted to do as long as someone else hadn't already been in trouble for it and gotten it written into the "don't do" book. John could always find a new way to do something.

John got up and walked to the one and only window in the outside office and stared down at the street below. In a couple of months his 20 years will be over. As he watched the action beneath him, he silently chuckled to himself as he gazed at the mass of civilians hopping from job-to-job. He knew that every time they changed jobs they started over; where he'd be retired before he hit forty.

John didn't exactly know where retirement would lead him, but for starters, he planned to build that Roadster he'd always dreamed of. A 426 Hemi complete with lots of chrome, rumble seat and, of course, red fuzzy dice hanging from the rear view mirror. He had it all perfectly in order in his mind. He figured it should take about a year to complete. It was his intention to use this project as a working vacation and as a pleasant transition from his fast paced military life into retirement.

"Admiral Benson will be with you soon, Commander."

He didn't have to turn around to know whose voice that was. Georgia Gray had been in this office for as long as John had been in the Navy. Ever vigil, ever loyal, Georgia. She deserved a medal herself for putting up with Charlie all these years. Loyalty was something John couldn't help but admire, especially since it was something that had apparently been lost in his marriage to Kate. He was still somewhat in shock from the little bombshell Kate dropped on him only five days earlier. No warning signs, not even a clue that there was something wrong. Just a "Dear John" letter left on the kitchen table that said she was leaving him and begging him not to try and find her. What the hell was going on.? The last he knew, they were both looking forward to retirement and, finally, the chance to spend time together without worrying about the phone calls that inevitably came in the middle of the night, taking him away and leaving her to wonder if he would ever return. No more tours of duty, no more calls to action and now no more marriage.? Jesus, it was driving him crazy.!

John knew he had to snap out of this depression he was in and focus on the subject at hand. For John had never, in his military career, mixed his personal life with business. After today, he'd have plenty of time to figure out just what he had done to end what he thought to be a life long relationship with the only woman he had ever truly loved.

Just as John was beginning to feel his blood start to boil again, the door to the Admiral's office opened and Admiral Charles Benson himself walked out to shake the hand of one of his best men and lifelong friends. Only today Charlie wasn't smiling.

Orders

The look on Charlie's face was all John needed to instantly know something big was in the making. He pitied the poor guy who would become the recipient of what lay behind those piercing blue eyes and that stone face.

Charlie didn't say a word when he shook John's hand and purposely led him into the privacy of his inner office. As the door was closed behind them, the silence was beginning to make John's skin crawl. "Jesus Charlie, you look like you just lost your best friend. The Boss giving you trouble or what.?"

"Something like that John, sit down and pour yourself a drink, then we'll talk, okay.?"

Of all the things Charlie could have said, this bothered John the most. For starters, it was just after nine in the morning. But most of all, John didn't drink and he knew that Charlie was perfectly aware of it. In fact, it had been a standing joke between them that of all the "bad habits" often found in servicemen; booze, cigarettes and coffee, John had chosen the least of the three evils. However, his lust for caffeine could be genuinely compared to the other two addictions.

Charlie, on the other hand, had developed a fondness for
Jack Daniels the likes of which you have never seen. He could
drink any two men his size under the table any day of the
week. John knew the offer was simply put as a deterrent to
what was really on Charlie's mind. The proof was in the fact
that John saw only one glass sitting next to the decanter on
Charlie's desk. And that glass looked like it had already been
used to contribute to the glow in Admiral Charles Benson's
cheeks.

"Okay Charlie, enough of the bullshit, sit down and tell
me what's going on. By the look on your face, somebody is
obviously getting shipped out and its not going to be R&R,
right.? Or are you drinking at nine in the morning because
you're so happy to finally be getting rid of me.?"

"You're right on one count, John. But I wouldn't be too
quick to put your oak leaves in a display case just yet, my
friend."

The smile on John's face was quickly replaced with one
of determination and forced control. "Don't even joke about
something like that Charlie. I'm out, done, finished.!" John
offered the papers in his hand, a postdated transfer to the
retired list and signed leave papers for the last fifty-eight
days he had left in the Navy. "I've given Uncle Sam my twenty
years and now it is my turn to get something back. So before
you start getting any bright ideas pal, you can just forget it.!"

"Now hold on John, don't get in an uproar. Just hear me
out. Something has come up. Something big. As of 0700 this
morning, all orders of leave are suspended and grants for
retirement denied. This comes from the top, John. There is
nothing we can do about it."

"The hell there isn't Charlie. My papers are in hand.
Signed, sealed and delivered. This ol' boy is history so don't
give me any song and dance about the brass because they
don't own me anymore.!"

John didn't realize until just then that he was shouting.

His hands were clenched at his sides and he could feel the cold trickle of sweat as it started its way from the base of his neck to the small of his back. If Charlie had been standing two feet closer, John had the sickening feeling that he would have punched him right in the nose. Not because he was angry with Charlie but because he now knew that the poor guy he was feeling sorry for earlier was not going to be a stranger. No, it wasn't going to be that easy. John himself was once again about to be asked to "do his duty for his country." Only "ask" is not a word found in the Naval vocabulary. But how could this be happening.? He was through. After a lifetime of service he'd given them all he had to give. What right did they have to ask for more.?

Charlie knew all too well what was going through John's mind right now. Out of respect for his friend, he said nothing more. He simply walked quietly to his desk, poured a generous shot of JD and sat down. He knew John would follow suit, (minus the booze), as soon as reality set in and he came to the conclusion that John Llewellyn was still Commander John Llewellyn, United States Navy.

With devout admiration, Admiral Charles Benson watched as his most valued officer came to grips with the fact that, for now, retirement was simply out of the question. As he filled his glass for the second time, that officer pulled up a chair and sat down.

The sailor who sat before Charlie now displayed nothing but professionalism. The tension in his body was gone. The expression of anger had been replaced with one of acceptance. The drastic change in John's demeanor would have been almost frightening had Charlie not known the man so well. Like so many times before, Commander John Llewellyn was ready for orders.

Charlie reached for the intercom switch and asked Georgia if she would kindly bring some coffee for Commander Llewellyn. No more than a minute passed before there was a soft tap on the Admiral's door and Georgia entered carrying a tray that had undoubtedly been prepared well in advance of Charlie's request. The tray held a small pot of coffee and a plate of carefully selected pastries from the cafeteria downstairs.

Charlie knew that Georgia was very fond of John as well. She too had watched John grow from the boy that had left his father's farm in Colorado to become a Seaman Recruit (SR), to the officer who sat before them now. In fact, Georgia had at times taken extra steps to somehow always know where John was stationed and would send him "care packages" and a few brief letters when she could. She knew John had no living relatives and from the first time she had met him, she knew he was very special. In her own way, Georgia had somewhat adopted John. Oh, Georgia knew better than to form any emotional ties with the young men she met during her employment with the military. But, this one was special. She really didn't know why John stuck out over all the rest, but then, it really didn't matter. When Georgia Gray set her mind to something, nothing and no one could change it.

"Here is your coffee John. Strong, black and lukewarm just the way you like it. I also brought an extra cup for you too Admiral, just in case."

Charlie just smiled and nodded towards the corner of his desk as an indication of where she might set down the tray. The manner in which Georgia spoke to Charlie could only be compared to the manner found between a husband and wife. But, after eighteen years as Charlie's secretary, Georgia had earned that right. Besides, Georgia always knew when she could use that tone with Charlie and when she could not. A fact that did not go unnoticed.

Charlie knew Georgia herself intended to retire soon, and the thought of losing her was more than he cared to deal with right now. Especially with the knowledge that his office, as well as many others in the Pentagon, was about to be caught up in yet another whirlwind of strategic conferences if not out right talks of war.!

John and Charlie both expressed their thanks to Georgia and with a smile and a nod, she quietly left them to their business. As she walked back to her desk, soothingly patting John on the shoulder as she passed, she knew something big was going down and, as it had in the past, this knowledge brought with it a churning fear in the pit of her stomach. A fear she knew was for John.

John poured himself a cup of coffee as Charlie unlocked the top right drawer of his desk. As Charlie pulled out the manila folder with the all too familiar government insignia on it, John couldn't help but feel a twinge of excitement, if not anticipation, at the thought of another mission. As Charlie began the briefing, John realized he was beginning to actually like the idea that he still had a talent which the United States government was more than happy to put to good use.

Like so many times before, John's orders were brief and to the point. He was to depart Washington D.C. on or about 25 December 1989 to arrive Subic Bay, Philippines no later than 2359, 31 December 1989. He would then report to the Commanding Officer for further assignment.

As was customary for this kind of transfer, John would take a commercial flight out of Washington-Dulles airport and pick up connecting flights out of Los Angeles and Honolulu, en-route to the Philippines. He would eventually end up in Manila where he would then travel by bus to Subic Naval Base.

"Wish I could give you more to go on John, but at this stage of the game, we just can't risk any leaks. The less you know at this point, the better. Believe me, you will be briefed in full once you reach Subic."

John wasn't at all surprised. As was typical of almost every assignment he had ever received in the past, he knew he would be able to obtain more than enough information once he reached his primary base of operation. If he couldn't get what he wanted from his commanding officer, he had developed several other contacts over the years both in and out of government service. The best part of this whole situation was that John was being returned to the Philippines. He would not be viewed as a newcomer in Subic. His reputation had been established years ago both on base and with many of the locals. John knew he would have no trouble whatsoever should he find the need for outside information or assistance. Still, he couldn't help feeling a sense of frustration at being sent on yet another blind mission without a clue as to what might be unfolding and what he was expected to accomplish.

John accepted his orders and exchanged a few more words of small talk with Charlie. However, John's head was literally swimming and he knew he had to get out of there and think. He had approximately two weeks to get his personal affairs in order and prepare himself for the journey ahead.

Charlie hadn't even mentioned Kate, and for that John was grateful. Two bombshells in one week were just a little overwhelming at this point, and John had the feeling Charlie knew what was going on anyway. Charlie always had an uncanny sense about the goings on around himself and his men. He also had the mental fortitude to know when to involve himself and when not to. Even though they were friends, Charlie was also John's superior and John's personal problems were not a topic for open discussion. Although John knew if he'd wanted Charlie's help in locating Kate, all he would have to do was ask.

John stood up and shook Charlie's hand. "Gotta go now Charlie, I'll send you a postcard from Subic."

As John turned to leave, Charlie held firmly to his hand. "Take care my friend, and when you get back, I'll personally walk your retirement papers over and process them myself if

I have to. Hell.! Maybe when this one is over you'll finally have a drink with me."

"I just might do that Charlie, I just might."

John walked out of the Admiral's office and smiled at Georgia as she was fluttering around the office trying her best to look busy, but she was obviously distracted. When John looked a little closer he could see a pinkish tint to Georgia's nose and a slight puffiness around her eyes. He knew she had been crying and for the first time since he had met Georgia many years ago, John walked up and kissed her softly on the cheek before finally leaving the office.

Georgia smiled at John as he left. But, once the office door closed she slipped into the ladies room and broke into tears. She too had been elated with the fact that John was retiring and would no longer be put into harm's way. It was at that exact moment when she realized just how very fond of John she had actually become.

This young officer had been coming in and out of the Admiral's office ever since she had been working here. She had seen over a decade of his broad smile and contagious enthusiasm walk in the door. He had sometimes left elated, sometimes content, but always with a cheerful smile and a sense of adventure on his face. Georgia saw John as a modern day Tom Sawyer, full of mischief and curiosity. He was a man who loved the world and all of the beings who came along with it.

She made the decision right then and there that if John was forced to delay his retirement, then by God, so would she. That is, at least until this particular sailor returned home safe and sound.

John

A light mist of rain fell as John exited the Pentagon. At first, the air would be weighed down with an odor of grease, dirt and garbage that had been imbedded in the streets from the preceding dry days. But as the rain increased in volume and intensity, these odors would be replaced with a spring-like freshness that always made John reminisce about his childhood days in Colorado.

John had been raised in a quiet and simple life style, far from the intrigue and the hustle and bustle of city life. He had managed his family's farm near Colorado Springs, Colorado, ever since he was old enough to pick up a pitchfork. Not that farm life was easy. John and his father would rise early each morning. They would have a light breakfast of cereal and toast at the kitchen table before morning chores. Each of them had their daily routine. John would gather the eggs and put fresh hay into the feeders for their two dozen cows while his father would milk Bess and Beulla. John's mother, Gladys, would take last evening's and the morning eggs into the candling room so she could pull out the culls and sort the good eggs from the bad before taking them to the local market. John would watch her silently looking at each egg, cleaning it, checking for cracks and placing it in the proper container. Gladys would take the eggs to market on Tuesdays and Saturdays. Though John was in school on Tuesdays, he loved to ride to market with his mom for the Saturday delivery.

After morning chores, John's father would change from his dingy farmer's corduroys into his pristine Air Force blues. Farmer Leo Llewellyn would become General Leo J. Llewellyn . . . John loved to watch the transformation. His father had been an Air Force officer for many years. After years of being stationed in just about every military base in the world, he had finally been granted a semi-permanent assignment at Colorado Springs, better known as "The Mountain", where he would finish out the remainder of his military career. John's mother always made sure that Leo's uniform was pressed in the meticulous manner befitting an officer. For some reason though, the General's shoes always seemed scuffed and unpolished. John attributed this to the fact that living on a farm with its dirt roads and pastures did not leave much opportunity for keeping one's shoes polished and free of dust. Until one day when he heard his father talking to one of his fellow officers . . .

Leo Llewellyn was standing in the kitchen, drinking a cup of coffee when he was asked once again why he did not take better care to complete his polished appearance by taking care of his shoes. John's father had this answer:

> *"When I received my first star, I started to relax.*
> *When I got my second star, I relaxed even more. By*
> *the time I got my third star, there were not many*
> *people left who could reprimand me or tell me to*
> *shine my shoes anymore. It is simply a privilege I*
> *deserve and have taken advantage of."*

He also wore a hat that was fondly referred to as a "ninety

mission hat." That meant that you flew and the hat was permanently bent from wearing your headsets while flying. John's father had, in fact earned his stars and was very proud to be an officer in the United States Air Force.

John never really knew what his father did in "The Mountain", but always had a sense that it was something not open for conversation. John would watch his father leave for "the office" and then scurry to make it to his own school bus.

John liked riding the bus to school. Thirty-five minutes each way, just enough time to get most of his homework done on the way home. On heavy homework days there was always the morning ride to finish it, but the challenge was to get it all done before getting home. John never wanted his homework to interfere with the evening chores and the time he could spend with his family.

Gladys would always have supper on the table shortly after her "boys" returned home. This was the family meal of the day. Four o'clock sharp.! Pass the peas, pass the potatoes, and reflect on the joys and adventures of the day. John especially liked this part of the day. Sharing the daily family treasures, sometimes laughing so hard the tears would flow, and his cheeks would start to cramp. These were glorious days for John.

After dinner, John would clear the table and join his father in the living room for the evening news and a short siesta while Gladys finished in the kitchen. John and his father had tried many times to help in the kitchen but Gladys wouldn't hear of it. She'd simply remind them what the rule was.

"I don't fiddle in your barn," she said, "you don't fiddle in my kitchen." Thus it had been and thus it would be.

After their siesta, it was time for evening feeding and the gathering of the evening eggs.

Sometimes, John's neighbor Keith would come over and help move the irrigation pipes in the west field. Keith's family owned the entire section of land and leased the southeast forty acres to John's father. Forty acres was plenty for this family of three to manage. Keith's family just wanted to keep the west field from packing down from lack of use and John was willing to help care for it to help with his family's rent. He felt that it was something he could do by himself and this gave him a sense of pride and maturity in helping his family make ends meet.

Over the years, John and Keith had become great friends. They rode the same bus to school, shared classes and each had a personal stake in the west field. Keith's father had offered each of the boys half of the west field as a high school graduation present if they could keep it from going to seed. This was a challenge they were determined to meet.

And so life went for John and his family for many years. Then, one day in late Fall, 1963, the unthinkable happened. It seemed people in the government were going crazy. John's father hadn't been home since the President had been shot three weeks earlier. He had left for work that day and had not returned. Of course, there had been a few phone calls to assure them that he was well. But after each call John noticed a change in his mother that sent a chill through his entire being. Gladys was a strong woman, but the look of anticipation and longing was not something she had ever expressed in the past. John's father tried in each phone call to raise their spirits but he just had no idea when he would be able to return home.

Then, on October 28th, there was a knock at the front door. An Air Force Colonel was standing in the doorway with a young professional looking woman beside him. He introduced himself as Colonel Blakely. John recognized the name. Tom Blakely and John's father had worked together many times but he had never been to the house. The woman was introduced as Mary Shields from the Family Crisis Center on base. She was there to help break the news and offer help in dealing with the unexpected loss of John's father.

John never did learn what had happened to his father.

All he knew was that his father's body was flown into Denver and there was to be a private funeral with "all military honors" the following day.

At the funeral, there were only about a dozen guests and the Honor Guard. John recognized several of the people as friends of his father. A couple of them were old friends of the family. All but one were Air Force. All were military. There were no listings in the obituaries. This was a quiet, family funeral.

On the way home from the funeral, John kept reflecting on something his father had said a few months earlier. John had taken his father to the west field to show him how well the crop was doing. John could see the pride in his father's face as he surveyed John's field. He knew he had done well. In this rare moment, his father spoke with him of his military career and reminded John of his choices. There would come a time when John would have to choose. "The Air Force lives well," he had said, "but there is much more to consider. Don't let yourself get drafted. Make the choice of service for yourself. Please don't follow in my footsteps. You would be much better served along another path." John agreed to his father's wishes but was still curious about the conversation.

Life changed so much and yet so little after the death of John's father. John picked up his father's chores and was doing well in school. Keith's family looked in a bit more often but Gladys and John were carrying on pretty well.

John was ending his senior year of school. High school had treated him well. He was on the football team and had even been elected team captain. This was quite an honor since John was not the team quarterback. He was graduating with honors and UCLA was offering him a scholarship starting in the fall. All seemed bright for John's future.

Then, right around Easter 1969, John's world fell apart again. Gladys had never quite gotten over the death of her husband. She continued to manage the farm, with John's help. Her dedication to her husband's memory and to the raising of John was all that kept her going. Unfortunately, her heart was broken beyond repair and once John had reached an age at which she knew he could take care of himself, her heart just gave out. There was no pain, no long-term hospitalization. Gladys simply went to sleep one evening and never woke up. When John found his mother the next morning, he couldn't help but notice the look of peace and contentment that had settled on his mother's face and he knew she was where she truly wanted to be. John's mother was a religious woman and believed that when she passed on, she would be rejoined with her husband. John didn't know what he really believed, but from the look on his mother's face he could only sense she was right.

John stayed on the farm for a while and made every attempt to keep it going in memory of his father and mother. Keith moved in as his roommate and helped run the place. As time went on their friendship became even stronger. Then came the long conversations about the Vietnam War and the upcoming draft. Neither John nor Keith had attended college over the summer months. It was all they could do to keep up with the challenge of working the farm and keeping the west field in shape. Then one day Keith received a letter that simply started with the word "Greetings", and they both knew what would follow. Keith had been drafted into the Army. This brought to John memories of the conversation he and his father had a few months before his father's death and John decided to enlist. John and Keith were great friends but John knew the Army was not what he wanted. His father had asked him not to follow in his footsteps, so the Air Force was not an option either. For John, the Navy seemed his best bet. Keith went with John to the recruiting office. For the next few days, he and John worked day and night packing up and securing the farm. Keith's father had given John one year to decide if he was going to keep the place. If not, he would be forced to lease the farm to another family. But whatever happened, John was promised fifty percent of the west field to do with what he wished whenever he decided which path he was going to take with his life.

John and Keith bid each other a fond farewell at the airport. Keith was heading to Fort Ord to complete his basic training and John was on his way to the Recruit Training Center, in San Diego, California. Each had promised the other to stay in close contact and visit each other whenever they were granted corresponding leaves.

Boot camp was nothing at all like John had seen depicted in dramatic movies and novels. Either that, or he was just accustomed to the grueling days of early wake-up calls that at times led them into the evening when most other soldiers could all but crawl into their bunks to sleep for about four hours before starting the routine all over again. John's Company Commander was not the overbearing, foul-mouthed individual that the general public was led to believe existed. In fact, when maneuvers were over, Gunners Mate First Class, Gerry Stiles, would sometimes join his men for an evening of cards and camaraderie.

Letters from Keith indicated that his basic training had turned out to be just the opposite. Keith compared his Drill Instructor to the staunch and punishing Sergeant portrayed in the movie "An Officer and a Gentleman." According to Keith, he and his fellow officers were already planning a painful and slow demise for the poor man if they didn't get to the end of their eight weeks quickly.

Both John and Keith made it through basic training without incident and as luck would have it, both entered the field of radio equipment and secured communications.

As boys they had played the usual games of war and secret agents. They had even developed their own code of communication that had, on more than one occasion, driven their parents nearly crazy. John's father had bought them both walkie-talkies for Christmas one year and they would hide out in the west field among the tall stalks of wheat and pass codes of information to each other until one would find the other and "rescue him from his captors". The sheep must have been both confused and amused at the game. Over the years, their code became quite extensive and was something they would carry with them for the rest of their lives. Before leaving for their military careers, John and Keith promised each other to never forget their secret code so they could keep track of each other and covertly communicate with each other even if they were taken hostage.

Over time, their selection of military assignments would evolve into each of them working undercover for a covert arm of the military known as "MSG" (Military Support Group). They both left for their assignments in November of 1969 and periodically ran into each other, but most of their contacts were made via Keith's parents back in Colorado.

Over the years, John and Keith had done more than most in making sure they kept in contact. They had met in some very interesting places and had even worked on joint ventures from time to time. But, like many childhood friendships, their reunions became fewer and farther between. The last time John and Keith had seen each other was in 1984 when Keith had stood up for John as best man in his marriage to Kate. Keith had never cared much for Kate, but out of respect for his friend he never let his reasons be known.

There was also no love lost in Kate's heart for Keith either. She never did take kindly to anyone who had even a remote effect on John or who could monopolize any of the time she had alone with him. This was probably the primary reason why John and Keith had drifted so far apart. Only John would never know the true reason behind the animosity between the two most important people in his life. Kate had done everything in her power to make sure of it.

John and Kate

As predicted, the morning sprinkle was turning into a significant storm as John proceeded through the gates surrounding the Pentagon. He had to pick up his pace in order to reach the street and hail a cab before he became completely drenched. Just as John was about to flag one down, an official looking vehicle pulled alongside the curb right in front of him.

A very young, tall and lanky fellow jumped out from behind the wheel and ran to the curbside in order to open the door to the rear section of the vehicle. The young man then stood at attention, saluted and said, "Seaman Scott Towers at your service, sir. The Admiral has requested that you be transported to your choice of destinations, sir."

It was all John could do to keep from laughing at the sight of this poor kid standing in full uniform with his hat tucked under his left arm, leaving his practically bald head exposed to this gale, and getting completely soaked in what had quickly become a heavy downpour. Charlie sure was pulling out all the stops on this one, John thought. He also knew Charlie had called in a favor for this little venture because

Commanders just didn't receive transport of this kind. It
made John wonder even more just what was about to go down
and why it was so important to Charlie that John be in on it.

Rather than question the lad and risk the chance of his
catching pneumonia, John simply returned the salute and
entered the vehicle. "What the hell, Scott," he said, "let's go."

John caught the look of gratitude on the young man's
face as he shut the door and ran to get behind the wheel
again. "Where to, sir.?" Scott asked. John rattled off the address to his apartment on 42nd Street and sat back for the
ride home.

"Home," John thought. "Not exactly what you'd call home
anymore." John had only agreed to lease the place for a full
year because Kate said she was tired of moving around so
much. She wanted a place she could fix up herself. A place
where she could have friends over and be proud to call home.
John, on the other hand, had never been able to call any
place home that wasn't located in Colorado. He still had his
stake in the west field on Keith's father's land. It had been
his plan that, when he could retire, he would build his dream
home on their half of the field where he and Kate could live
out their golden years in the fashion his father and mother
had. But Kate had put her foot down this time. She said that
she had been a good officer's wife for five years. Never staying
in one place long enough to hang a portrait or pick out
curtains. She made John promise that they would stay in D.C.
for at least a year before picking up and moving again. John
knew how hard military life had been on Kate, and out of love
for his wife, he had agreed.

John knew Kate was nothing like his mother and never
would be for that matter. Kate was of a different breed. She
had been raised in money and society all her life. He had
often wondered just what had really drawn them together in
the first place, but in his heart of hearts, he knew.

John met Kate at a dinner party held in honor of Charlie's

birthday in 1984. Kate had arrived in the company of her father, Ronald Dupree, a wealthy businessman and close friend of Charlie's.

All heads turned, including John's, when Kate walked in on the arm of her father. She was a knockout.! Her golden hair fell just to the middle of her back. Her eyes were sky blue and held a sparkle you could see from across the room. Supporting that height was the most beautiful pair of legs John had ever seen in his life. Her height of 5'11" did not intimidate John, for at 6'3" himself, he had met very few women who he could look at eye to eye without having to adjust his line of vision. This 'Kate' had his attention. The chemistry between them was instantaneous and John was more than infatuated before the night's end.

John watched for a while as a multitude of men made every attempt possible at striking up a conversation with her. His own courage was boosted when he noticed that every time he looked across the room at her, she was looking back. About two hours had passed since her arrival before John decided on his approach.

Kate's father and Charlie were engulfed in a rather serious conversation and Kate had made herself scarce by stepping out on the verandah. John excused himself from the group he was involved with and walked outside to introduce himself. There was no awkwardness in their introductions to one another and from the moment they first spoke, there was never a lull in the flow of conversation.

John and Kate spent the rest of the evening together. They talked, danced and politely mingled with the other guests. Kate introduced John to her father. As he shook John's hand, he looked at his daughter and smiled, which John took as an implication of his approval.

By the end of the evening, John was so enraptured that he regretted having to say good night. Kate made no attempts at being coy and, before leaving, she placed a small slip of paper with her telephone number on it in John's palm as they shook hands and said goodnight.

John couldn't remember ever having such an immediate reaction to a woman like Kate in his entire life. He couldn't stop thinking about her. The way she smiled; the way she smelled; and the way she felt when he had slipped his hand around the small of her back while dancing. He hardly slept all night for thinking about Kate. The very next day he placed a call that would eventually lead them into marriage.

John and Kate spent every lunch and evening together for three months. Their relationship was like a romantic novel, full of picnic lunches, candlelight dinners and moonlight walks on the beach. They shared childhood memories and dreams of the future. Kate appeared to hang onto every word John said, especially when he talked about his life in Colorado. She had never experienced the freedom of country life and had in fact been raised in a very strict household only to be followed by "proper" boarding schools. These, according to her mother, would mold her into a "proper young lady" of which her father could be proud. Kate always had a gleam in her eye when she talked about her life at boarding school. As Kate put it, "boarding school was anything but proper." Between the midnight runs to meet the boys from prep school, to experimenting with what was known at the time as "recreational drugs", Kate had managed to keep up with her studies and had graduated with honors. She was the apple of her father's eye; demonstrated by the enormous allowance she was provided and the many expensive gifts she was given on a regular basis.

John knew Kate was spoiled and wondered often if he was getting into a situation in which he couldn't keep up. Officer's pay wasn't peanuts, but it wasn't anywhere near what Kate was used to having at her disposal. Before he had time to really let this fact become a genuine concern though, John was hooked.

John asked Kate to marry him at the beginning of the fourth month in their relationship. He had orders for yet another mission and he did not want to leave Kate behind without his promise of marriage. Kate was beautiful and intelligent, but she was also very insecure when it came to relationships. John came to the conclusion that this was because her father had been gone for the better part of her life and she knew that on several occasions, he had strayed from her mother's bed. She was always afraid she would never see him again. Kate said she would only be able to wait for John if she were his wife. She knew John was the type of man that would never stray if he had a wife waiting for him at home.

They were married two weeks before John was to ship out. Keith flew in for the occasion in order to be John's best man. Keith had met Kate on a couple of other occasions and had strong reservations about John's decision to marry Kate, but he wouldn't miss the honor of standing up for his best friend no matter what the issue. John would later wonder why his best friend arrived so late and left so soon after the ceremony.

Life with Kate was like most marriages. It had its ups and downs. The downs came every time John shipped out. When he would return, it seemed to take longer and longer each time for Kate to warm up to him again. It was as if she thought of his career as a betrayal to their love, like the Navy was taking him away from her instead of providing him with the means to make their life a comfortable one.

Of course Kate never had to worry about finances. She still received an allowance from her father, unbeknownst to John who thought the arrangement had ceased. John had in fact asked Kate's father on several occasions to stop the monthly "gifts" (as Kate's father put it) and allow him to support his wife himself. Kate had a very bad habit of venting her frustrations at John's absence by spending days on shopping adventures. It never failed to surprise John, each and every time he returned home, at the new little treasures Kate had picked up while he was away. John knew Kate hated being alone and that this was her way of staying busy. He also knew that eventually one of them would have to get used to a little different lifestyle if they were ever to have a truly committed and happy marriage.

Kate was just beginning to come around to John's point of view during the past year. At least it seemed so to John. Only now he had to wonder just what she had really been up to. What had really triggered her leaving and just where in the world had she gone.?

John snapped out of his daydream just as the car was pulling up in front of his apartment building. The rain had let up for the moment but the dark clouds that lingered brought with them the promise of more to come. John didn't wait for the driver to come around and open his door for him. After all, enough was enough. He thanked Scott for the transport, returned the young man's salute and entered the building.

John had rented the second floor of an impressive old brownstone just outside of D.C. It had been Kate's choice of course. This way she was just minutes from downtown and could travel by cab to her choice of destinations if John was working since they only owned one car. Kate's father had offered to buy her a car of her own but on this issue, John held firm. One vehicle would be hard enough to ship when they moved back to Colorado, let alone two. Kate had balked of course, but after two days of pouting, she had finally come around to John's way of thinking.

John climbed the flight of stairs that would lead him to the private entrance to the second floor apartment. As he entered the foyer, the emptiness in the place hit him like a ton of bricks. The first thing John set eyes on was one of Kate's prized sculptures. It was of a man and a woman embraced in the act of lovemaking and without thinking, John reached for the statue and threw it across the room. Of course it shattered into a million pieces but even this futile act didn't bring any calm to the rage that was progressively building in John's mind. It did, however, bring him to the realization that he wasn't just going to lay down and accept Kate's disappearance. He had less than two weeks in which to find her or find out just exactly what had happened to drive her away without so much as a hint as to why she had decided to end their marriage.

The two weeks came and went. Kate had simply vanished, with the exception of her note, without a trace. She was no longer in Washington, nor was she in contact with her parents or any of their friends . . . just gone.

DC≠Manila

It was an unusually warm morning for January in Washington as John headed for the airport. He had neither been able to find Kate nor make contact with Keith in his final two weeks before departing to the Philippines. Kate was a very well known woman and it was amazing to John how well she had managed to leave without a trace. None of their friends had heard from her, no phone calls, not even a charge on her portfolio of credit cards. Nothing.

Keith was a whole different matter. It was fairly common to lose track of this creature of the shadows. In his line of work, a low profile often came in handy. John knew Keith would show up. The question was . . . when and where.?

This was the kind of flying John could get used to. In-flight movies and hot meals weren't part of the flight profile in Navy cockpits. Usually a flight started with an hour of briefing and another hour of pre-flight checks on the aircraft, followed by sitting in a hot cockpit for another half-hour waiting for your turn on the catapult. That's where the real fun began.

Strapped in, buckled up and pointed towards the front

of the ship. Ten stories in the air and nothing ahead but open ocean. Engines to full power, final instrument check, salute and WHAM.! SWOOSH.! There's no better way to wake up in the morning than from trying to relocate your eyeballs to the back of your head with a hot catapult shot. Unless it's with a cold cat shot. That's when you barely make it off the front of the ship, dropping most of those ten stories, and hope you can get up enough speed to climb out of there before you hit the water and get run over by the aircraft carrier. Yes. In-flight movie, stewardess, flushing toilets, stereo, snacks . . . this was MUCH better.

It was a wonderful day for flying. John enjoyed seeing the farms in the Midwest with their circular fields, optimized for maximum efficiency in planting, irrigation and harvesting.

John thought to himself, "These fields were nothing like the forty acres at home. John plowed with an old John Deere tractor and planted by hand. The tractor wasn't pretty, but it was as regular as taxes and Aunt Mildred".

Los Angeles came and went. A quick plane change and it was back in the air, headed for Hawaii. John had hoped for a layover in Honolulu but found himself getting right on another plane headed for a short layover in Guam and then on to the Philippines.

John kept drifting off. Half awake, half asleep, he couldn't help but daydream of his first visit to . . .

Guam, Nov. 1974.

John is stationed at the naval base in Guam, attached to the commodore's staff embarked on the submarine tender pier-side in Apra Harbor. Vietnam is winding down. Saigon is about to fall. There is a massive evacuation in progress from mainland Vietnam. Refugees are being transported from the Vietnam coast to Guam . . .

This was an interesting few weeks for John. He had been temporarily assigned to the nuclear submarine USS Snarkfin for patrol off the coast of Vietnam. His duties were to assist in the detection and cataloging of radio transmissions along the Vietnam coast. Many SOS calls had turned out to be attempts to lure US ships into unsafe waters where they would be easy prey for shore based artillery.

John's team was to detect, localize, validate and assign priority to these transmissions. His team had been assigned to a submarine primarily for security reasons. All surface ships in the area were taking on refugees for transport to Guam. Since refugees were unlikely to try and swim down to a submarine, it seemed about the best bet for this kind of operation.

At the height of the evacuation, John had been assigned to the number two periscope to monitor surface activity. On one of the heaviest evacuation days, the Snarkfin thought they had hit a whale. The officer of the deck ordered Snarkfin to periscope depth to take a look around and then intended to surface to check for possible damage. John was just returning from the radio room when the officer of the deck asked him to keep a lookout on the number two periscope. What John saw would stick in his memory for the rest of his life.

As the Snarkfin approached the surface John was able to take a good look around through his periscope. That's when he saw it. Dead ahead. The aircraft carrier Snarkfin had been shadowing for the last three days. The flight deck looked like an old discarded candy bar covered with ants . . . thousands of them. Helicopters were swarming around like honey bees around their hive. Suddenly the officer of the deck barked out the order, "Right full rudder—ahead full."

John took his eyes out of the periscope to see what was happening. He looked at the officer of the deck who had been on number one periscope. The OOD caught John's eyes and said, "Keep your eye on the helicopter on the port side of the carrier." As John watched, two more helicopters landed on the carrier. Then he watched as the carrier crew pushed the first helo over the edge of the flight deck. John reported that the chopper was clear of the deck and in the water. It wasn't until then that he realized what had happened.

Aboard the carrier the helicopters were arriving full of refugees. They were landing on the flight deck and didn't have enough fuel to make it back to the mainland. If the ship had taken time to refuel one of the helicopters, three others would run out of fuel and have to land in the ocean. They were simply landing the helicopters, evacuating the passengers and crew, then tossing them over the side to make room for the next bird to land. It wasn't a whale they had hit at all . . . It was one of the sinking helicopters. By this time Snarkfin was well away from the back of the carrier . . . and a bit less in harms' way.

As damage reports came in to the OOD it became apparent that they had lost their radio antenna as a result of the mishap. The Captain had the crew rig up an emergency antenna and used the carrier to relay our condition to the Commodore . . . they were ordered to return to Guam for repairs.

A few days later Snarkfin pulled alongside the tender in Apra Harbor. Boy was John glad to see the sun again. This submarine stuff didn't agree with John much. To him submarines were fine as long as they stayed in the pond at Disneyland.

As soon as Snarkfin tied up alongside the pier, John reported to the Commodore on the tender. This was John's first encounter with Commodore Bradley. He seemed sociable enough. He sort of looked like a marine in miniature. Razor sharp creases were in his heavily starched khaki uniform. Straight as a ruler from the floor to his shoulders. John, standing 6'3" in his bare feet, was standing in front of a man whose shoulders barely reached John's waist. Now John knew why behind his back people called the Commodore, "Bitsy Bradley". All 4'7" of him . . .

The Commodore listened to John's summary of the mission and thanked him for bringing him the information so quickly. Then he changed the subject. "Charlie tells me you haven't been stateside in nearly four years John. You're more than due. Why don't you stop back by tomorrow once you've had a chance to clean up and get some rest." John thought it was a pretty good idea and thanked the Commodore for his concern on the way out.

In keeping with a very old (and equally questionable origin) tradition, the crew of the Snarkfin immediately departed the boat for a barbecue at the park just past the end of the wharf. Submariners relish this "coming home" party after being underwater for weeks or months at a time. Nothing special. Just hot dogs, hamburgers, and cold beer. The difference is . . . the hot dogs and hamburgers were barbecued over a grill. Aboard the submarine everything was microwaved so the smoke wouldn't pollute their air. And beer . . . Oh . . . ! To be a part of the New Zealand Navy where they still had a daily ration of rum . . .

John joined the party shortly after leaving the Commodore. As was normally the case, the tender crew already had the grills fired up and the meat a roastin' by the time the Snarkfin crew came down the gangway. This is where the stories fly and friendships are renewed. And there, flipping burgers like hotcakes, John saw Willy.

John had known Chief Wilson for several years. It seemed as if anytime there was any kind of action going on . . . Willy was there. They had met in San Diego at the Recreational Services Boat House. John and Willy were both avid sailors and Willy was teaching the Red Cross sailing course. Willy was a pretty fair sailor, but his eye was always watchful to spot a new bikini on the beach. This particular day, John was at the boathouse looking for a good workout. John had heard of Willy by reputation and thought it was about time they met.

John introduced himself (catching the gleam in Willy's eye when he heard John's name) and asked if any of these planks were able to leave the dock. Willy, having heard of John's reputation as a sailor, said he could take his pick but he'd have to take a check sail in order to take a boat out on his own. John saw the smirk hiding behind Willy's half smile and knew this was to be a fun check ride.

They took Willy's 18' catamaran for a quick trip around the bay. John had rigged the boat while Willy watched looking for any sign of weakness in John's seamanship skills. He was still looking as they left the dock. That's when Willy made his first mistake . . .

Willy had noticed a new bikini on the beach and in a

moment of weakness said "Lines are free. Let's see what she'll do." John, taking advantage of Willy's distracted attention, pulled in the sail real hard and the boat lurched forward as the sails caught the wind. As the sail filled, the windward hull came out of the water and the boat was off like a shot from a cannon. Willy, on the other hand, had been paying more attention to the girl in the bikini than to his own handhold and found himself treading water alongside the pier as John and the boat sped off along the shore.

John turned around and picked Willy out of the water. Only Willy's pride was bruised but the stage was set for a great day sailing on the bay. They spent several hours sparring with each other that afternoon and came away quite the best of friends.

John walked up behind Willy at the barbecue pit and said in a quiet voice, "I see you're still treading water." Willy spun around to see John standing there with a huge Cheshire grin. "You old sea snake, how are you.?" They spent several hours getting caught up and sharing sea stories 'til Willy had to "go to work." John asked him what he was doing to keep off unemployment and Willy simply responded, "Baby Lift."

Operation Baby Lift was the processing of Vietnamese refugees for entry into the United States. The Navy had set up a huge city of tents at Orote Point on the other side of the harbor. John was fascinated and asked if he could help. Willy replied, "The more the merrier." And off they went . . .

It was amazing. Hundreds of tents and thousands of refugees were all huddled onto a piece of land about the size of two city blocks. There were rows and rows of people sleeping along the sides of the tents. Some had a small bag of their belongings to use as pillows. Most had lost everything in the evacuation.

Bright and early the next morning, John was up and about. Happy as a clam for he knew what he wanted to do for the next few weeks. He was looking forward to his morning meeting with the Commodore. But not for the same reasons as when he had left the day before.

John arrived promptly at the scheduled time for his appointment with the Commodore. The Commodore's aide whisked John in like royalty to a wedding. The Commodore had great news. He had talked with Charlie last evening and John was scheduled for the afternoon "milk run" back to the States. John's disappointment was more than apparent.

Commodore Bradley was a bit surprised at John's reaction to the news. He couldn't help but ask if there was something wrong. John shared his wanting to help these people and his desire to stay and help with their processing if he could. "I have no family left and many of these people have none either. In a way, if I can help them, it would make me feel a lot better. I would really like to stay for a while." The Commodore understood and arranged for John to be assigned to the processing unit for 60 days before his transfer back to Washington. John was a happy man.

John was assigned to work at the reception desk processing refugees. One evening, while taking a break for a snack and a soda beside the processing tent, John was approached by an older Vietnamese gentleman with a rather unique, and interesting, proposition . . .

The gentleman was traveling with his daughter and fifteen-year-old granddaughter. The gentleman told John of his concern for his granddaughter's safety. She was young and innocent, yet her future was uncertain. He had been watching John for several weeks as he processed many of his countrymen into the United States. He had come to trust John for being gentle and honest with the people he had processed. Now was the moment of truth.

Mr. Ng had noticed John was not wearing a wedding ring and asked if he had a lady back home waiting for him. John had dated several young women but, as yet, hadn't found one willing to wait for him. And then it came . . . Mr. Ng asked if

John would marry his granddaughter and take her back to the States as his wife. John had seen young Miss Ng and knew she was a beautiful and loving young lady, but marriage . . . ? Mr. Ng immediately felt John's hesitation. "Of course there's always her dowry," as he handed John a heavy metal bar. About the size of a chalk eraser but the weight of a bowling ball. John realized this was a bar of solid gold being offered as dowry.

John's head was spinning. It wasn't every day he was offered a lifetime with a woman as lovely as Kym. Nor was it a daily occurrence to be offered a fortune in gold. John returned Mr. Ng's dowry and asked if he could think about it for a day or so. Mr. Ng agreed and offered that it might be a good idea for John and Kym to get to know each other a bit better. John thought it would be a good idea also and for the next few days John and Kym were inseparable.

John learned of her family who had lived just outside Long Xuyen near the shore of the southern flow of the Mekong. Both of her brothers had been killed in the war as had her father and many of the men of her village. Their family had managed to distance themselves from much of the politics of the war. Only with the fall of Saigon had they fallen into serious jeopardy. Each hour they were together, John and Kym found themselves being drawn into a relationship that would last far beyond this time of tents and broken lives.

John knew he was building strong feelings for Kym. He and Willy had talked several times about the Ng family. Little did John realize, Willy had seen the solution days ago.

Where was Willy.? He had been courting Kym's mother. Willy was always looking for the bargain. The deal to end all deals. And suddenly here she was. Sitting on his knee was Lotti. She was Mr. Ng's daughter AND Kym's mother. If Willy married Lotti, all three of the Ngs could go back to the States with him when he transferred next spring. He still wasn't sure about the marriage part. But, what the heck, he'd never tried it so what was there to lose.? He figured he might even get a few home cooked meals out of the bargain.

"*Sir. Would you please fasten your seatbelt and bring your seat to the fully upright position.? We are on approach to Manila.*"

John was smiling when the flight attendant woke him for arrival in the Philippines . . .

Manila=Subic

John liked this part of traveling to the Philippines. Catch the bus from Manila to Clark Air Force Base. Wait around Clark Air Force Base awhile to see if you could get a hop-out to Diego Garcia with the Air Force, or drop down to Subic Bay, cross the bay to Cubi Point Naval Air Station and catch one of the Navy flights out. Orders generally take you through the Air Force routes because there are regularly scheduled military airlifts. Of course, on this trip he still hadn't been briefed. For John's purposes Subic Bay and Cubi Point were the places to go. With this in mind, John walked out of the airport looking for the bus to Subic.

"Hey sailor, looking for a date.?" John would know that voice anywhere. There he was, across the street sitting on the hood of a . . . whatever-you-might-want-to-call-it. It looked like a Jeep, but it was made out of stainless steel. There were fuzzy dice, red and gold dangling ornaments, an unbelievable assortment of chrome and . . . no muffler. The natives call these taxies. Tourists come to know them as "Jeepne". Whatever you may call the vehicle . . . the ornament on the hood was . . . . Keith.!

Keith and John gathered up bags and jumped into the Jeepne for the trip to Subic. "Be happy you're out John. Be happy you're out of The States. The dung is about to hit the fan."

What a strange thing to say, John thought. The rest of the trip was spent speaking of home, the West Forty, and how the family was doing. The sort of normal things friends talk about while they're traveling together. Nothing was really said about John's orders or why he might be in the Philippines, or on his way to the Indian Ocean for that matter. John just knew it was good to be back with an old friend. The only thing Keith had to say to John on the business side was, "Watch your six. Be careful who's behind you." Keith could see that John had heard this and it was the end of the subject.

BOQ

Keith dropped John off at the Bachelor Officer's Quarters in Subic Bay. The Subic Bay Officers' Quarters was one of John's favorite places. He loved to hang out here. Suddenly, Keith looked up and said, "Gotta' go. Remember, watch your back. This could get pretty ugly before all is done."

More confused and curious than ever, John carried his bags inside the officers' quarters. The ritual began. John immediately dropped his bags at the front desk, walked through the small door to the right of the check-in desk and put his name on the chalkboard. The chalkboard is the reservation board for the massage house that's part of the officers' quarters. John returned to the front desk and checked in to his room for the evening. As always, his room was waiting, a ground floor room in the "Red" wing. All good sailors are familiar with the term, "Red-Right-Returning". Being put up in the Red wing was a sign of respect. New people are always checked into the Green wing (which also seemed appropriate to John) until they either earned Red wing status, or leave the Philippines having never been invited to the privilege. In his room, John dropped his bags and returned downstairs for an hour of massage.

What a wonderful way to unwind from a continuous flight from the states. Twenty minutes in the sauna and a cold shower can relieve many of the things troubling mankind. But John knew there was more to come.

It seemed like hours, waiting there on the table for the masseuse. John's mind kept slipping back to Guam . . . and for good reason. Just then the silence was broken by the curtain as it opened, revealing one of the most beautiful women John had ever seen.

"Putting on a little weight aren't we sailor.?"

"Yeah, and there's a lot more gray these days too." John was now sure there was a heaven, and that he was in it. Life just didn't get any better than this. "It's been a long time. How are you, Kym.? And how's your father.?"

"Life's been good until lately. People are starting to get a bit too crazy for me these days, especially the last month or so. I think they're putting something into the water. Something dark and sinister . . . Not to mention fattening. Pop wants to see you. Soon."

"What's going on.? People are acting like someone dropped the new kidney transplant on the operating room floor. Everyone's looking at everyone else as if to say 'I can't believe you did that', and then getting sheepish when others notice them noticing."

"I don't know. Nobody's talking. And EVERYBODY's making sure everyone else is aware that they would notice if something *was* said. I don't know, it just doesn't make sense."

John realized that this was not an invitation to an office call, this was a request for a private meeting. John knew what he needed to do . . . After his massage, John dressed and headed for town.

John made the trip into town crossing over "Shit River". What a change since the last time he was here. John remembered seeing the young girls in their gowns, jumping from boats to retrieve quarters that were being thrown into the water by onlookers on the bridge. . It wouldn't have been so bad, had it not been for the mucky-brown color of the water and the fowl stench coming from the river. Apparently the Admiral's wife had put her foot down and Public Works builders had put up plywood walls on both sides of the bridge. Now you couldn't even see the river. The days of quarter diving were a thing of the past . . . Probably for the best . . .

John turned left at the end of the bridge, going down back roads where most people don't dare venture, to a little bar out in the middle of nowhere. This place was not one to be writing home about. It was a sleazy front facade with a young woman sitting in a window calling down to passers by . . . Business was obviously slow, with only an occasional new passer-by and people who had been to town many times before.

John walked in the front door, sat down at the end of the bar and asked for "Mama San". An older lady walked up to John at the front of the bar. He greeted her warmly and asked to use the bathroom. She told him where the bathroom was and reminded him to use the second men's room on the right. John strolled to the back of the bar and went through the hanging curtains. As instructed, John went to the second men's room on the right, and entered Shangri-La.

It was like entering another world. There were marble floors, lace draperies and more jade knick-knacks than a person could imagine. This was the "inner circle", the place tourists never see. To most who visit here, the Philippines seem dirty and barely civilized. This was the other side of the "P.I.", a sanctuary . . . but only for a select few. John was among those few.

"Welcome John. It's been a long time. Sorry to hear about Kate." Whew, news sure travels fast in these circles. John hadn't even come to grips with Kate's disappearance and already it was common knowledge on the other side of the world.. A funny time we live in.

"Hello Willy. Kym said you wanted to see me. What's up.?"

"You tell me. There's more back scratchin' and toe sniffin' goin' on than I've seen since Watergate." "I heard Charlie kicked you out of Washington. Did you know Keith is in town.?"

"Yes. He drove me down from Manila. He kept telling me to watch my back. The whole trip was pretty strange. Do you know what's going on.? Is there something I should know about.? Am I in some kind of danger that I'm not aware of.?"

"I don't think so. Everyone is acting pretty spooked. Something real big is getting ready to happen. Sorry, but I haven't been able to find out what yet. I was sort of hoping you could tell me. I guess we're both gonna' stay in the dark for a bit longer. Can you stay the night.?"

"Only if I'm still welcome. The last time I was here you threatened to orphan me after my squadron whipped your base basketball team sixty-three to eight."

"Had to bring it up again didn't you. Well, even orphans need a place to get in out of the cold. Anything you need.?"

John knew this was an offer to provide an escort for the evening but Kate was still in his heart and on his mind. "No, thank you anyway. Maybe another time.." They both knew a one night stand was never John's cup of tea. Then again, it was always nice to know he was worth the offer . . .

Morning came all too soon. John was awakened to the smell of fresh coffee and a warm hand running through his hair. He could smell the fresh scent of Ivory soap and feel the warmth of a woman snuggling behind him. "Good morning Kym."

"Good morning, John. I didn't mean to wake you." Kym had arrived soon after John had gone to sleep and decided not to wake him but wanted to be sure to be there when he woke up. She knew he would be leaving early and she might not otherwise get a chance to spend any time with him, especially considering the way people were behaving lately. She thought he might get wrapped up in . . . whatever it was . . . and not get back to see her for a very long time.

After curfew lifted, John returned to the base and reported to the Admiral's office for presentation of orders. John's visit with the Admiral was like a revolving door. In one side of the office, "Here are your orders Commander", and out the other door. Not exactly a 'social' call . . .

"Proceed from Subic Bay, Philippines to Diego Garcia, British Indian Ocean Territory (BIOT), for further transfer. Report to Commander Task Force Seventy Eight for follow-on assignment. "

That's it.? No final destination.? Briefing will be in Diego Garcia.? Only questions. No answers. John thought this was beginning to play like an old record . . . 'Round and 'round but getting nowhere fast . . . There had to be a better way . . .

"The Air Force milk run leaves at noon. They are holding a seat for you. Good luck, Commander"

Hmm . . . Talk about the 'bum's rush' . . .

To Diego Garcia

The news of an Air Force flight was a mixed blessing. It would be nice to be on a flight with flushing toilets and an in-flight meal. It's even nicer to be able to stretch out on the cargo bay and catch up on some sleep. But there simply wouldn't be any time to snoop around for more answers at Subic.

John arrived at the air terminal to find the flight crew waiting for him. As it turned out, the plane had been loaded the night before and the crew was ready to depart ahead of schedule. This was one of the Air Force maneuvers to avoid having to take passengers. Unfortunately, their flight clearance was being held until John was on board. Even though John was over an hour ahead of scheduled departure, the flight crew considered him "late" and were a bit grumpy about the delay.

John presented his orders and the flight was given immediate departure clearance. The pilot welcomed John and thanked him for being so early. "Usually we have to wait another hour for departure clearance and end up getting delayed another half hour trying to get the passengers situated. It's nice to have you."

Once in the air, John found a comfy little spot to lay down and dozed off thinking of Kym . . .

John and Kym had become very close in John's last few weeks on Guam. For the first time since his mother died he had been having feelings of family. It was a bit disconcerting that Willy could have ended up as his father-in-law, but such are the quirks of life.

On his last evening on Guam, John took Kym out to a wonderful dinner and dancing at one of the hotels in Tamuning. It was a wonderful evening. There was romance in the air. There were many honeymooning Japanese newlyweds staying in the hotel. Tamuning was to the Japanese as Honolulu was to newlyweds from the States, a great place to vacation and honeymoon.

Kym knew John had to leave the next morning. She knew she would see him again but she wanted to share something special with him. On the way back to the base, Kym had John pull over on one of the beach overlooks to look at the stars and listen to the surf. There were few words. They had all been said. Kym pulled close to John and whispered, "I have something for you."

Kym handed John a small but finely wrapped package. Inside he found a small gold and coral pendant. She told John the gold came from the bar he had been offered with her hand. The coral had come from the live reef on the south side of the island. It symbolized a piece of the place where they had met. The design of the pendant had been handed down through her family for generations and only the finest of craftsmen could duplicate it. Her grandfather was one of the last and had worked on it for weeks, day and night, to have it ready for this evening. Kym slipped the pendant around John's neck and kissed him on the cheek. She said her grandfather had made two, then gave him the complementary pendant and had him put it around her neck. They were two, each different, and each perfectly complementing the other. When placed together they fit perfectly, yet each stood on its own. They agreed it was a perfect gift.

"Commander, we're starting our approach into Diego Garcia. Approach Control has asked that you report to Base Operations upon arrival."

"Rolling out the red carpet I see.. Thank you. And please thank the rest of the crew for me in case I don't have a chance to thank them in person after we land."

John tucked the pendant back inside his shirt and prepared for arrival.

Dodge

"Welcome to Diego Garcia, Commander. I am Ensign Kendall. I hope your flight was comfortable. There is an Intel briefing in about an hour. The British and Base Commanders will meet you in the briefing room in fifteen minutes. . You may leave your bag here and I'll see it gets to your quarters for you. Airman Jones will escort you to the briefing room. Is there anything else you need Commander.?"

"I think you have it all covered. Thank you."

Now this was a bit more like it. The last time John was in "Dodge" was eighteen years ago when there was nothing here but a Navy Weather facility. Today there were roads, buildings and even a runway. Quite a change from coming ashore on a rubber raft..

When John entered the briefing room the British Commander greeted him at the door. The Base Commander joined them a few minutes later. John presented a package to the Base commander which he had hand-carried from Subic.

"Commander, you will be staying the night and departing tomorrow afternoon for Oman. From there you will be transported to the aircraft carrier where you will become US Liaison for Littoral access to the Persian Gulf. Your duties will include regular Littoral access flights to all countries bordering the Persian Gulf in support of the Carrier Task Group. As you know, we make regular flights to all of these countries in order to exercise the diplomatic channels, which allow us to get our planes in and out in time of crisis. Admiral Benson has briefed us on your background and we are quite happy to have you here."

"I'm happy to be here, Sir. As you know, I have yet to be briefed. Would it be possible to meet with Intel to get brought up to speed on the region.?"

"The Intel briefing in a few minutes is for you. We normally do Intel briefings only on Mondays, but you will be in the Gulf by then. We thought you might like to know why you've been flown half way around the world on such short notice. Ah, here's Intel now."

"Good day, Commander. I am Lieutenant Thompson. I will be conducting your briefing and have been authorized to provide you with any information you need. This briefing will be in two parts. The first session will be a general briefing, and update, open to flight officers and operations support commanders. The second session will be limited to the Intel community due to the classification of the material and its sensitivity. Shall we get started.?

Lt. Thompson took the podium and called the briefing to order. "Good morning. Activity in the Persian Gulf region has remained active since our last briefing. There has been an increase in activity in a rural community approximately eighty miles to the southeast of Baghdad. This activity has been characterized by numerous caravans of trucks, apparently moving materials in and out of this rural community. There have been . . . Blah . . . Blah . . . Blah . . . "

John had heard most of this on the TV news. The activity in Iraq and the response from neighboring countries was getting its share of news time but no more than any other region of conflict in the world. There had to be something more to this than what was being briefed . . .

". . . This concludes today's briefing. Next briefing will be on Monday. Thank you for your attention."

Lt. Thompson gathered her notes as her assistants started 'cleansing' the room of classified charts and photos. "Commander, if you will follow me, I will take you to the vault where we can continue your briefing." It had been a while since John had been given this kind of treatment. In Washington there were officers, senior to him, who spent a good portion of their days getting coffee for Admirals and Senators. It was nice to be back in the real world, where being a Commander seemed to have a bit more meaning.

The vault was just that. It looked very much like the bank vault where his family stored things like the car titles and insurance papers. The walls were probably two feet thick and covered with acoustic tile. Other than a dozen steel filing vaults, everything was in plain view. There was a place for everything, and everything had a specific place. This was standard practice in this type of environment. If anything was moved or tampered with, it would immediately look out of place and draw attention.. Simple, and effective.

"Commander, your clearances and need to know have been validated. The rest of this briefing is Top Secret and above. Please treat the information accordingly." John understood. Lt. Thompson closed and secured the vault door and continued the briefing.

"Sources have revealed that the materials being shipped into the rural community mentioned in the previous briefing are consistent with materials necessary to manufacture biological weapons. Another facility has also been getting an increase in truck traffic. The materials being shipped through that facility are consistent with the manufacture of chemical agents. Both facilities appear to be processing material in large enough volume to support a war. To date, the processed agents appear to be remaining inside the borders of Iraq but the stockpile is becoming substantial."

The briefing lasted almost two hours. There was no longer any doubt as to why Charlie wanted John as his eyes and ears in this matter. John had many friends and contacts in Saudi Arabia, Oman and other countries in the region. If anyone could get the 'real' picture, it would be John.

John finally understood why this had been kept so quiet, or at least so he thought. If the general population of the world were to learn that they may be in danger of being poisoned in their sleep, there would be mass chaos. NOT a pretty picture.

This was a lot for John to take on. His mind was reeling at the thought of someone releasing chemical and biological weapons on their neighbors. It brought to mind pictures of the Holocaust and Hitler. Not to mention atomic bombs, and Japan. John never had been able to understand why people couldn't just let each other alone and be good neighbors. But there always seemed to be a bully who wanted to make their point of view, the only point of view, to survive . . . regardless of the cost.

It was lunchtime by the time all the briefing was completed. John was invited to join the group for lunch and asked if he would like an island tour that afternoon. What a great idea. Maybe seeing some of the island would take his mind off the pictures of tragedy in the making he had been shown all morning.

After lunch John checked into his room and changed into something a bit less formal than his uniform. After all, this was a tropical island. It was in the mid-90s and the sun was almost directly overhead. Shorts were definitely in order. Lt. Thompson knocked on John's door and he opened it to find a rather pleasant surprise. Was this the same Lt. Thompson who had been briefing him all morning.? Take away the wash khaki uniform and the lock step unemotional presentation, add a sun dress and a smile, and you end up with Lisa Thompson. A cross between fashion model and the girl next door. This was looking up to be a much nicer afternoon.

Lisa had arranged to use the duty vehicle to take John on a tour of the island. There was so much to see, and so very little time to see it.

It took about an hour to drive to the farthest point on the island. Lisa showed John the old plantation and what remained of the old weather detachment facility he had visited almost two decades before. The building was still standing, but barely. Most of the equipment had been removed but there were remains of the old diesel power generator and the "plumbing" system. Since power was in very short supply, running water was a bit of a challenge. Rainwater was collected from the edges of the roof and ran through plastic pipe into a holding tank just below roof level. Pipes then ran from the bottom of the tank into the kitchen and bathroom. As long as it rained every three or four days there was plenty of water for the facility's needs. More than a few days without rain meant using the outhouse on the other side of the camp. A few more days without rain would lead to washing dishes in saltwater. At least there was a semi fresh water well for drinking water when the need arose.

John could still remember his first trip to this facility. Then it had been manned by a crew of six, who often didn't get visitors for months at a time. Now the camp was deserted and mostly reclaimed by nature, only to be visited by an occasional hiker to ponder its past. Somehow it seemed fitting that the British had decided to limit access to this area of the island and preserve it as a testimony to the island's history. The Brits had always been rather fond of history . . .

Also preserved were the old cemetery and loading house. The loading house had just been given a fresh coat of whitewash by a group of volunteers. It looked pretty good from the outside, but could barely stand on its own, as was the state of most structures left standing on this part of the island.

The cemetery still had its 'bleeding table' intact. This is where they would place the body of someone who had died, and drain it of its fluids before burial. The picture of this table in a dark overgrown place brought chills to both John and Lisa. Just then there was a rustling in the bushes. Lisa and John both nearly came out of their skins.

"Hi Molly," Lisa said when she recognized the visitor as one of the islands wild donkeys. There were about a half a dozen donkeys and, supposedly, a horse roaming the out-reaches of the island. The horse seemed to be more fable than fact, but Molly was real enough.

Lisa pulled an apple from her backpack and offered it to Molly. This had to be 'Donkey Heaven' for Molly, perpetual play time with her donkey friends, only broken by visitors bearing gifts of food and scratching her ears. . . . Heaven indeed . . .

Lisa and John toured the island for most of the rest of the afternoon. They stopped at a spot on the inner lagoon for a quiet picnic and talked about island life. Special Services was a very important group on the island. Most people get stationed in "Dodge" for a full year. During his or her tour each person was allowed two weeks off the island. Other than that, the island was their home for the full year. For this reason, Special Services got treated much better here than most other overseas stations. There were sailboats, windsurfers and catamarans for checkout, as well as classes to learn how to operate them. There were two power boats that took people out on half-day sport fishing trips, a bike shop, two gyms, three theatres, an assortment of clubs, and of course the "Brit Club".

The Brit Club was unique on its own. The island was actually an extension of Mauritius. The Brits had a long-term lease and the US sub-leased it from the Brits. An interesting arrangement since all there is on Dodge is a US Navy base and Air Station. Of course, there was the handful of British Marines stationed as the island's caretakers and they needed a place to call "home". The Brits had a small compound, which was considered British territory. All who were invited there (the Brits invite everyone) could enjoy life under British rule as long as they remained in the compound. This position got tested from time-to-time when two people would decide to go on a date to the Brit Club. The US Navy has some pretty strict rules about "fraternization" but the Brits don't see the need for such restrictions. As long as the couple is on "British Soil" the rumor is there's nothing the US can do about it . . . So the point got tested from time to time.

Periodically, romance would blossom and a couple would decide to get married. This made life interesting (or a nightmare) for many, since married couples were not allowed to be assigned to Dodge at the same time.

The situation was usually resolved by allowing the chaplain (the only marrying authority on the island) to take the couple through their vows on the afternoon, or evening, before the first of the newlyweds would be leaving the island. This was wonderful because the couple was able to get married abroad, but awful in that they may have to wait months before their partner could transfer, and they could start their honeymoon. Imagine getting married and having to wait six months for your wedding night . . . !

Ah.! Ha.! . . . The supreme test of the virtues of having the sanctuary of British rule over the Brit Club compound..

Oh.! Britannia.! . . .

. . . Of course the smart ones just made sure the non-transferring partner managed to take their two-week, off-island, leaving on the same plane as their transferring spouse. Thus, Singapore became a popular honeymoon destination, since it was often the first refueling stop on the way back to the States.

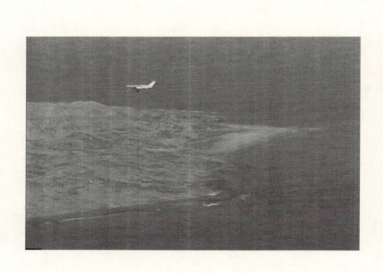

Driving to Oman

It was raining when John awakened. Most days on Dodge had at least one shower this time of year. The day started with two hours in the island gym followed with a hearty breakfast in the galley. The Ship's Store opened about an hour before John was due to leave, which allowed him to pick up some last minute requests for the people forward deployed in Oman. There weren't many flights between here and Oman but each crew tried to take along items the Oman Detachment had requested. Usually it was one of the passengers who was designated to retrieve the items and hand-carry them to their final home. This left the flight crews free to concentrate on their primary task of getting the plane safely from one place to another, a concept John had long appreciated.

The flight to Oman was long and boring. It was fifteen hundred miles, all over water and not a single point of land in between to check your navigation. On the up side, even if your navigator totally loses it, you can always just watch the sun and keep driving north. Eventually, you would get to land. The only challenge would be to figure out WHERE you were when you got there. If you ended up too far west, you would be in Yemen. Not a great place to try and land a US military airplane. The best course would be to turn right and follow the coastline. Eventually you would run out of land and have to turn left around the coast of Oman. Most of our pilots knew this point of land and could negotiate the rest of the trip to their destination by the seat of their pants. The challenge was to not get shot down in the process. The Omani aren't real trusting of aircraft approaching their coastline unannounced or unidentified.

This trip was the first overseas navigation flight for Ensign Carver. He was fresh out of navigation school and the crew was interested to see how he would stand up to the pressures of "real" overwater navigation. All too often new navigators miss the 'big picture'. Navigation is a lot like the weather. Even the best predictions, and most careful attention to detail, periodically needed a bit of a reality check by simply looking out the window. That time came soon enough. As we approached the coastline, Ensign Carver predicted our position relative to the airfield within one half mile. When the accuracy of his prediction was announced, you could hear the groans all the way into the cargo bay. The crew had taken up a pool based on the new ensign's predicted accuracy. The best anyone had predicted was that he could get us within FIVE miles. Not bad for the first time out of the chute. It looked like this crew had picked themselves a winner . . .

John checked in with the Operations Coordinator for information about his hop out to the aircraft carrier. His hop was due to land and refuel just after dawn the next morning. It was to be a hot swap of crew and cargo. The off-going crew would turn over the aircraft to John and his new co-pilot and remain ashore for transfer back to the States. John had actually expected to get all the way to the carrier at least before he picked up a new flight crew. At least his first takeoff in the Gulf would be from dry land instead of being hurtled off the pointy end of a boat and hoping you stay in the air.

Oman was a rare treat for John. He always liked coming here. This was a very small community. It was an Omani airfield with a few Brits stationed here just to keep things interesting. There were seldom more than two US flight crews on the ground at the same time. It was one of the rules the Oman government had put in place to keep their little station from becoming a full-blown base of operation for foreign militaries.

Coming to Oman was like getting a mini-vacation. There was a wonderful galley with fresh bread made daily and served hot, right out of the oven. Things like imported orange marmalade and occasional pate on the tables evidenced the Brit influence.

John put his things into his assigned room and headed out to the perimeter fence to visit his friends. As he was leaving the compound, Ensign Carver saw him and asked if he could tag along. "Of course" John said. "I'll introduce you to some of the local charm. You wouldn't by chance have any cardboard would you.?"

"As a matter of fact, there is an empty box in my room. Why.?"

"You'll see. Let's grab a few pieces before we head out." They each tore off several pieces of cardboard and then headed to the fence.

"Are you ready for a treat.?" John asked. "I remember the first time I came here. A crusty old Omani officer brought me out to the fence. It was an experience I've never forgotten. Look. Here they come now."

Ensign Carver turned to the fence expecting to greet one of John's Omani friends. As he turned, John could see the young ensign's jaw drop in amazement. Instead of people, there were two tiny camels approaching the fence.

"Ensign, I would like you to meet my friends. I call them Oasis and Dates. Most people have their own names for these two, so feel free to either borrow mine or come up with a couple new names of your own." John held out a piece of cardboard to each of the camels. They walked right up to the fence and ate right out of John's hand.

"That's a great trick Commander. How did you get them to be so friendly.?"

"There's no trick to it at all. They just like the cardboard. Actually, I think it's the glue that holds the cardboard together that's the actual draw. An old guy who worked in the transportation garage introduced me a few years ago, so I come out here most every time I get into town. The camels seem to enjoy the feeding and I enjoy bringing it to them."

"But they're so small. How old are they.? If you've been coming here for years, they aren't babies. Will they get bigger.? Where are their parents.?"

"Hold on there Ensign. Slow down a bit. These are normal sized adult Omani camels. They just don't get any bigger here. The parents are still around and do come by to visit from time to time. In fact, I saw them just a year ago. Guess they didn't know I was coming to town and already had another commitment. Here, have another piece of cardboard for Oasis. I'll feed mine to Dates."

John and Ensign Carver walked back to the compound and cleaned up for dinner. Every evening was special at dinner in Oman. The cook had once been a chef at a very well known restaurant in Hong Kong. An "unfortunate misunderstanding" had made it unlikely he would ever be welcomed back to Hong Kong so he had migrated to Oman. Now he made a point of creating "special" meals every evening when there are visitors in town. It wasn't clear whether the meals were intended to keep the chef's skills up or if the special meals were a way of advertising, in hopes of someone offering him a job, and thus VISA sponsorship, to a country in the Americas or Europe. Either way, the food was w.o.n.d.e.r.f.u.l.

After the evening meal, everyone retired to the TV lounge, which served as the theater. There was a larger than normal crowd this evening because it had been almost two weeks since the last movie. Video players didn't seem to last long in this sand and grit-filled environment. Their operational life was somewhere between six and eight weeks. The last machine had only lasted a month, which eliminated movies until a new machine arrived from Dodge. Since John had been the courier, he was asked to pick the movie and given a front row seat. There's more than one way to get on the Welcome Wagon . . . John knew it wasn't because of his looks.

John really became the man of the hour when he pulled out a copy of *Hunt for Red October,* which had just been released. He was supposed to be taking it to the officers' mess on the aircraft carrier. John didn't think a little sneak preview before going to the boat would hurt anything. He was right. The chef even cooked up a huge batch of popcorn to underscore the occasion. After all . . . even the operational boys on the boat hadn't seen this one yet . . .

Across the I/O
and into Kuwait

For the next several months, John was truly in heaven. Every other day he would make a trip to one of the countries surrounding the Persian Gulf or the Sea of Oman. There were also occasional trips to Diego Garcia and some of the countries surrounding the Indian Ocean. Seventeen countries in as many weeks . . .

John especially enjoyed the trips to La Reunion, a little island to the south of Madagascar. The Hotel Bourbon was pretty standard as hotels went but the service was wonderful. In St. Denise there were some of the best French pastry shops in the world. Everyone was friendly and hospitable, the kind of place where he would like to settle down and raise a family.

There were so many wonderful people and beautiful places to visit. Sometimes it was hard to remember this was all part of John's "official duties". Of course the "official" part was in exercising the diplomatic channels which enable American planes to fly into these countries. Then again, the

photo safari near Nairobi, feeding camels in Oman and visit-
ing the United Arab Emirates certainly made the trips a lot
more interesting.

John even managed to go to the international vacation
islands known as the Seychelles. As with all the other trips,
there was the "official" element. In this case it was for Sea Air
Rescue. A small fishing boat with three men had been missing for three days. John and his crew were diverted to the
Seychelles because they were enroute from Diego Garcia to
Somalia and happened to be "in the vicinity".

John spent nearly four hours searching to the north of
the Seychelles before landing with no sign of the missing
fishermen. Not long after daybreak the next morning, they
were in the air again. About three hours into the flight, one
of the observers in the back of the plane spotted something
floating. A little closer look proved the sighting to be, in fact,
the missing boat.

John made radio contact with a Seychelles fishing trawler
and vectored them to the small boat. The crew of the trawler
picked up the small craft but the boat was empty and adrift.
The only sign of the fishermen was a note carved into the
seat with the message, "Please tell my wife my last thoughts
were of her and our love.". . . a message John would never
forget.

John and his crew continued their mission to Somalia
the following morning. A quick overnighter in Mogadishu
and it was off to Jeddah in the west of Saudi Arabia. This was
an especially interesting place for John. So close to the tur-
moil of Jordan and the West Bank, yet life here seemed so
normal. The people were friendly and social. It was more
like home than a foreign port. The biggest decision of the
evening was to determine which video they would rent and
who would go out to the video store to get it. This could have
just as easily been an evening at home in Colorado.

The next morning, as they started the day's pre-flight of

their aircraft, they were redirected to Kuwait City, Kuwait. There was an American oil drilling consultant who had become ill and needed whole blood for an operation. The blood had been located in Saudi so John and his crew were to pick it up and drop it off in Kuwait on their way back to the ship.

The trip was uneventful but John's crew was tired. They had been on the road for nearly three weeks straight without a break. A car from the hospital met the plane to pick up the cargo. John and his crew were treated to lunch in appreciation for their quick response.

As John was about to leave the restaurant, he ran into an old friend. Omar was the local coroner and teacher of human anatomy at the hospital. He was also a long time contact for John. This could be John's chance to finally find out what all the intrigue was about. It was an opportunity John needed to take advantage of.

John asked his flight engineer to take a long hard look at a fuel leak and sent the crew to start the preflight checks while he made a quick stop at the hospital with Omar to check up on the patient.

At the hospital John learned that the operation had gone well and the patient was in recovery. Good news was welcome to lighten the thoughts of a crew which was still dwelling on the events in the Seychelles. Omar invited John and his crew to stay the evening and John admitted he had hoped for the offer. John told Omar there was a fuel leak on one of their engines and that he had asked the flight engineer to take a close look at it while preparing for departure. Fuel leaks are common occurrence on most aircraft. John knew it was a good way to delay for repairs a day or two if necessary. This could be one of those times when the combination of a tired crew, a marginal fuel leak and 'other factors' would justify spending the night. It would allow them to land rested in the daylight instead of attempting a carrier landing at night with a very tired and fatigued crew . . . At least that was John's plan . . .

There was a fuel truck alongside when John returned to the aircraft. Normally this would not get John's attention, but the last leg of the flight should only be about an hour and a half. If anything, they were a bit heavy already and might have to burn off extra fuel in order to land. Taking on more fuel just didn't make sense. John had also expected the flight engineer to ground the aircraft because of the fuel leak.

As John climbed aboard the navigator handed him a message . . .

"Carrier group in radio silence. Position significantly different than briefed. Proceed immediately to Diego Garcia. Report to station Commander for further tasking.

Charlie"

"Commander, we have topped off on fuel and the aircraft is ready for departure. I have a secure channel with Admiral Benson. He wants you to make contact right away." The Navigator handed the headset to John.

"Good day Admiral. We were about to return to the carrier."

"Sorry to throw you another curve John, but I need you to go back to Diego Garcia."

"Sir, we only have two more flight hours left today. It's over six hours to Dodge. The crew has flown maximum days five times this week and we have a fuel leak on the starboard engine. I recommend we delay departure until daylight in the morning."

"I understand your concerns John. The situation is such that I need you to leave Kuwait immediately. If safety of flight dictates, you are authorized to stop in Oman on your way south, but I need you out of Kuwait immediately."

"Understood."

This was more than simple direction to fly to Diego Garcia. There was something more. First off, Charlie was hard line on not violating maximum daily flight hours. Secondly, Charlie had addressed him as "John". Not "Commander" but "John", on official channels. This was a first.

John proceeded to address the crew . . ."Attention to brief. We are departing immediately for Diego Garcia. I realize we are almost out of flight hours for the day but our orders come directly from Washington. Daily flight maximums have been lifted for this flight. As soon as we are clear of the coast, I want everyone to get some rest so we'll be alert for the night approach into Diego Garcia . . ."

Fifteen minutes later . . . they were in the air, on the way back to Dodge.

Back to Dodge

"*Navy 524, Diego Garcia approach*"

"*This is Navy 524*"

"*Navy 524, You are cleared direct Diego Garcia. Report ten-mile marker. Upon arrival, Flight Commander and crew are to report directly to the Base Commander for debriefing.*"

"*Cleared direct Diego Garcia. Report ten-mile marker. Roger.*"

It had been a quiet flight back to Dodge. The sky was clear and the stars, like flowers in spring, were in full bloom. Most of the crew had managed to sleep at least part of the flight. Everyone was looking forward to a couple days off in Dodge. The crew was starting to run a little short on things like deodorant, clean clothes, and rest.

Lt. Thompson met the aircraft with a van for the crew. "Welcome back Commander. Looks like you're a bit more of a rabble-rouser than I had thought. They're all waiting for you in the briefing room."

"They.? Who is, "They".?"

"Everyone. The Base Commander, Operations, the British Commander, . . . everyone. You sure know how to throw a party", she said with a wink.

John was either WAY too tired or totally confused. Either way, he was not looking forward to debriefing with the brass after logging over seventeen flight hours in the past twenty four. And this was just a repositioning flight. No special tasking. Just move the airplane from Kuwait to Diego Garcia. No big deal . . .

The Operations Center looked like party headquarters an hour before the polls closed on election day. People were frantic. They were practically running from one place to another. Some had looks of determination, others concern, and a few looked just plain . . . scared.

"Lisa, what's going on.? Are you having some sort of drill.?"

"So you don't know.?"

"Know *WHAT*.?

"About half an hour ago, Iraq invaded Kuwait. Kuwait City is under heavy fire. We thought you could bring us up to date since you just left there."

"What I left was a quiet city, where I had just eaten the best meal I've had in a weeks."

"Oops. Wait right here."

Lisa disappeared and returned a few seconds later with the Base Commander. After a few minutes of private debriefing, John and the crew were released to go get some rest. They were given twenty-five hours off and then would be heading back to the Philippines.

John stopped by the lobby on the way to his room. On the television, there were already 'Special Reports' commenting on the developments in Kuwait. This wasn't just a border skirmish. It was a full out invasion. No wonder Charlie wanted him out of there in such a hurry. This was the second time Charlie had chimed in without warning and pulled John's bacon out of the fire.

Lisa dropped by to let John know Maintenance had found the fuel leak on his aircraft and expected to have it repaired in a few hours. She also brought a pizza. Had it been any other occasion, John might have been more receptive to Lisa's obvious invitation. She was a lovely woman—tall, attractive, good-natured and obviously very bright. Their first meeting had been more like a reunion than an introduction. Almost as if they had known each other for years. Lisa could be some-one John would like to get to know a lot better . . . when the time came.

Lisa and John had pizza, took in the midnight movie and enjoyed each other's company. Though it was a very short visit, John knew he had a new friend. A friendship he hoped would last for years to come.

The next day, it was back into the aircraft and off to the Philippines. None of the crew had done laundry, gone shop-ping or any of the other things they would normally have done on a stop like this. After all, they were on their way back to Cubi where you could have your laundry picked up in the evening and get it back on your doorstep before dawn, with proper military creases, for about a dollar per uniform. It was a bargain anywhere. Of course, you only sent out half of your laundry at a time. The service was typically great, but every once-in-a-while, something would find itself missing. Under-standable, considering the nightly volume, but none-the-less a bit awkward if you lose all of your clothes and have to fly out of the country the next morning.

Normally flights returning from Dodge make an over-night stop in Bangkok, Thailand or Singapore in order to refuel and get a bit of R&R. Not this trip. This time they were carrying the courier pouch, which precludes any such stops. The lack of an overnight stop was received with mixed re-views. Some of the crew were disappointed to miss an evening in Thailand. Most were happy to be going back to Cubi. John was just tired. According to the rules, the crew had flown so much in the last thirty days they needed to see the Flight Surgeon, to be certified safe to continue flying. With or with-out a flight waiver, this crew was entitled to at least three days off when they landed in Cubi. Everyone agreed, the sooner they get to Cubi, the sooner they would get a little time off. Morale was high.

While on approach into Cubi, John saw something that would change his life forever . . .

Cubi=Keith
Spills the Beans

"Commander, look over there.! Our ship is sitting alongside the dock at Subic."

"You think that's odd. Look over there.! Our relief is tied up at the other end of the shipyard.!"

John knew right away there was something wrong with this picture. Our aircraft carriers always did their turnovers and transferred the guard while ON-station in the Sea of Oman or in the Northern Indian Ocean. There hadn't been a day without a US Carrier Task Group in the Indian Ocean for over two decades. This was getting better by the minute.

After landing in Cubi, John and the crew checked in with Operations. They were to all go through the formalities of seeing the Flight Surgeon, 'just in case', and then they were to get four days off the flight schedule. This was welcome news to a very tired crew.

John checked into quarters and went to sign up for his

massage. Keith met him at the door. "Hello John. Feel like grabbing a beer.?"

John left with Keith and headed to Willy's. It was actually just a short trip into town. Over the river and about four blocks more. But oh, how the climate changed in those four blocks. This time it was serious.

At Willy's, Keith gave John an earful. "Did you notice anything different about your arrival John.?"

"As a matter of fact, yes. How is it both carrier groups are in Subic.? That means there isn't anyone in the Gulf. We haven't broken coverage in the Gulf for, probably, twenty years."

"Good observation, John. Remember the last time you were here.? You knew I had been working on anti-terrorist support for several years. What you didn't know is that we had a very serious problem late last year. Remember the bomb scare in San Francisco.?"

"Sure, they thought there was a bomb in the Trans-America building. It turned out to be some kid's science project in the trunk of his mother's car. Didn't she turn out to be some high-powered corporate executive or something.? Things seemed to get pretty quiet from there. I just thought it was damage control so she didn't sue."

"Yeah. It made for a pretty good cover. Actually, what if there really was a device found. What if it wasn't a bomb. What if we found several quart-sized containers containing a very powerful biological agent. If released from the top of the Trans-Am building at the right time, the wind would have carried it throughout the Bay and probably all the way to Salinas, killing every living thing in its path."

"I knew there were such agents, but I didn't know any had ever been found outside the labs."

"Think about it John. You could get enough agent to take out Los Angeles, New York or any of a dozen other major cities into a package the size of a can of hair spray. Once released, it becomes airborne and kills everything in its path

until it dissipates in about three days. Someone could eliminate a population of millions in a matter of a couple days,
and leave all the buildings, freeways and other infrastruc-
ture intact." "Do this to one or two major population centers,
and the threat of being able to repeat the act any time and
any place could shift the balance of power and control of an
entire nation."

"Pretty spooky stuff Keith. But this is hypothetical, . . .
right.?"

"Of course, John. But think of it. Most every major city has
a perfect launching place. The Trans-Am building in San
Francisco, the World Trade Center, the Seattle Space Needle.
The list goes on and on. A woman could carry it onto an
airplane and Security wouldn't give her a second thought.
What's so special about a woman with a can of hair spray in
her luggage.? Or a kid with a can of soda.?"

"So what does this have to do with Kuwait, Keith.? We're
talking mortars and tanks. Not to mention the fact that it's
two countries, half way around the world from the US."

"Sure, John. But what if we followed the agents back to
their source.? And what if that source were to be in the Gulf.?
Wouldn't it be nice to cut off the problem at its source of
production rather than chasing it all around the world.?"

"But it still doesn't explain Iraq attacking Kuwait. And it
certainly doesn't explain two carriers in Subic."

"John, do I have to draw you a map.? Think about it. We
couldn't just go in and start bombing Iraq for no apparent
reason. That would be international political suicide."

"So you're saying we brought the carriers out of the Gulf
in order to invite Iraq to invade Kuwait. That way Iraq is the
bad guy, and we get to go to Kuwait's rescue. In the process
we manage to take out Iraq's ability to manufacture and store
these weapons even before they try to sneak them across
borders."

"Well, I must say, you are finally headed in the right
direction."

"So, why are you telling me all this Keith.?"

"You were sent here to be Charlie's eyes and ears. I was sent here because I know too much. Knowing too much has a tendency to shorten one's life span. Just in case something should happen to me, I thought it would be nice if someone else knew what it was all about. Hell, Willy thinks I'm here to look into Commissary and Exchange items getting off base into the black market. Like that's something new . . ."

"So you're saying we're getting ready to invade Iraq.? That's crazy.!"

"Have it your way, John. I'm just a crazy old farm boy. But, think about what I've said. It may shed a different light on what's happening."

It was indeed a lot to think about . . .

TWO Carriers in Subic

Subic was in chaos. Normally there would only be one aircraft carrier and her support ships in-port at a time. This put a few thousand Americans at once using the combined facilities of the base and the town. This could prove to be a bit "testy" from time to time, but there was generally enough room for everyone. TWO carriers and their accompanying entourage was simply a mess.

John took the chaos to his advantage. Flight crews and ship's company generally stay aboard their ships when the carrier pulls into port. Sometimes the privilege to go ashore and stay in the barracks is extended to some of the crew, usually as a reward for outstanding performance.

Flight crews will sometimes fly their aircraft off the ship prior to entering port. This allows the option of using the aircraft for shuttles and to pick up parts, which aren't available at the local base but are critical to get the ship back underway. The nice part of being one of these crews is being able to stay ashore with your aircraft.

This was John's lucky day. The confusion of having two aircraft carriers in port would let John get a little snooping done. The carrier would know he was staying ashore, and the base would have him registered, but think he was actually on the ship. He would really spend all his time out at Willy's so he could use his three days R&R to check in with his civilian resources without drawing any attention.

The rumor mill was all a buzz. There was more under-cover work going on amongst John's resources than in the local brothels (which were also pretty busy with TWO carri-ers in town at the same time). Unfortunately for John, most was more rumor than hard information. He did find out there was a lot of activity at Clark Air Force base and that it had been spooling up for a couple months. Other than that, there simply wasn't much new going on.

Kym had decided to take some time off also. The base was crazy busy and there were plenty of others who wanted to do "meatball massage". Kym mostly worked with her "regu-lars" who appreciated getting a quality massage without hav-ing it turn into a solicitation. They all knew Kym was a profes-sional masseuse (and a very good one) and not in another profession using the same title.

John had always been a bit concerned about Kym's ca-reer choice. He would remember back to Guam when her grandfather offered him a small fortune to protect her from such situations. Kym's grandfather had died several years ago, but his teachings and values lived on in her.

Kym was an anomaly. Vietnamese by birth, she lived and worked in the Philippines with her adopting American fa-ther. She worked in a field often populated by prostitutes yet she had never taken a man. Kym portrayed herself as being a common run-of-the-mill girl but she was very well educated with a Bachelors degree in Chemistry and a Masters in Busi-ness. And she was beautiful to boot. John didn't envy many men, but the man who married Kym would certainly be an exception.

Kym escorted John for three days as he touched base

with several of his Philippine contacts. They drew very little attention when together. Most anyone seeing them would assume they were a couple and that she was simply showing him around the country. John liked the mobility this arrangement afforded but didn't care much for people thinking she was his "escort".

Besides drawing very little attention, they also drew very little new information. At least everyone was singing the same tune. The common theme was that Kuwait was invaded in order to grab their oil. Nobody believed the US would roll over and let Iraq continue to occupy Kuwait, there was simply too much world impact because of the oil reserves involved. There seemed to be concensus, war was eminent and the US would be a key player.

Nothing, absolutely nothing, was even mentioned about nuclear, chemical or biological concerns in the region. This was the only piece that seemed out of place . . .

Back to work

John's stay in the Philippines was a welcome rest from the hectic pace he and his crew had been maintaining for the last couple months. Now it was time to go back to work. The carrier task group had left for the Persian Gulf just twenty hours after John had arrived in Subic. The crew had been left behind to let them recover from their last month of excessive flying and as a means of ferrying last minute parts to the ship while she was in transit to the Gulf.

Their time was up. The last of the critical parts had arrived at the supply depot and they were immediately scheduled to deliver the cargo to the ship. The ships had been gone for three days. John and his crew would fly to join them in only three hours. Oh, the wonders of modern technology.

This would be a long flight day for John and his crew. They were to fly to the carrier, drop off their parts and continue on into Saudi Arabia. Not a real hard day's work, but the Admiral would be going with them.

Life always got interesting when the Admiral flew with you. Like any place in life, everyone gets a bit edgy when the "boss" is right there. As it so happened, this particular Admiral was a pilot. This meant he could take command of the aircraft at any moment. It also meant he had the right to actually fly the aircraft. This thought always made the crew a bit nervous. Though they had the right to fly, most Admirals didn't exercise the privilege because they didn't want to reveal how out of date their flight skills had become.

This flight was an exception to the rule. The Admiral would be flying most of the trip. As it turned out, the Admiral had never flown an S-3 and wanted to get "oriented". The nervousness was evident in every crewman's eyes. As the Admiral and his aide boarded the aircraft, the Admiral's aide whispered a comforting bit of information to John . . . Admiral "Buzz" Bradley had once been a test pilot assigned to NASA. John just looked up and thanked his mother for making him say his prayers every night. One of them had just been answered.

Buzz was a friendly sort. He elected to fly from the co-pilot's seat and mostly left the plane on auto-pilot. This in itself was a great comfort to John because it meant they would not have to change seats in flight in order for John to make the carrier landing. Admirals were allowed to do a lot of things but none would be foolish enough to try a carrier landing at night, in an aircraft they had never flown before, even if they were allowed to do so by the regulations.

It was a beautiful night for a carrier landing. As they approached, they could see a light green phosphorescent trail that started about a mile behind the ship and took them all the way in. The Admiral remarked, "Either this is something right out of *The X Files*, or Dorothy settled too soon when she followed the yellow brick road. She should have seen this. Either way, life just doesn't get much better than this."

John smiled his agreement as they took the #2 arresting wire and came to a stop on the carrier deck. Quite a night indeed . . .

John and the crew were aboard the carrier for nearly two hours. Everyone had a job. John spent most of the time getting briefed on their trip to Saudi, the Flight Engineer readied the aircraft for departure, the Navigator was briefed on radio frequencies, flight clearances and other associated details while the Ordnanceman helped with the off-going and on-coming cargo. It was a well-oiled machine.. This crew worked very well together and John was proud to be part of it.

The second half of the flight went just as smoothly as the first. An easy launch and smooth weather made for a wonderful flight. It was when they were approaching the northern coast of Oman that they got their first sense of what had happened. They could see the gray-blue haze coming from the burning oil fields in Kuwait all the way down to the Gulf of Oman. There was a glow on the underside of the haze layer coming from the fires on the coast of Kuwait.

As they approached the United Arab Emirates, the smoke and haze kept getting thicker making it harder and harder to maintain good visibility. If they had been flying in US airspace, they could have altered their altitude much more easily to stay within pockets of cleaner air. That wasn't an option in the Persian Gulf. Flight clearances were slow in coming because everyone was being cautious. Flight crews had to be extra cautious as well, because the sky looked like the Louisiana Bayou with aircraft clearance lights mimicking fireflies zooming in all directions. This could easily get out of control.

At dawn they were given their clearance to cross into Saudi airspace. The crew had been holding off-shore for nearly an hour, but it had seemed like a year. The air smelled so fowl, everyone had been intermittently putting on their oxygen masks to get a little relief. It was sobering to experience this flight environment. The vacation was over.

The Jeep

The next month or so made for some pretty interesting flying. John and the crew made it into almost every country in the region. India and Pakistan were great to visit and Sri Lanka had wonderful spices catering to John's desire to learn more about the finer points of being able to cook for himself. The idea was to find a way to make microwave food taste more like something from mom's table. John quickly realized it wasn't the spices, it was the love that makes for wonderful eating. In fact, it didn't have much to do with the food at all. But every little bit helps . . .

It wouldn't be long now. England, France and many other countries had all sent troops and an amazing array of hardware into the region. Even if there were not a Kuwait, there would certainly be conflict. You simply can't put this many troops, from so many countries, in the same place, at the same time, without something happening. It was only a matter of time.

The Internet was abuzz. A jeep with two American observers had been overdue. The jeep had been recovered but there was no sign of its occupants. This was not a good sign. Now the conflict was getting personal. It wasn't just a matter of the regional bully overpowering one of its neighbors. Now it was two Americans missing right in the middle of things.

John kept a pretty close eye on what was appearing in the news. Especially some of those tiny articles nobody else seemed to even notice. There was a report of the Coast Guard boarding a cargo ship heading into the Gulf. The Zanoobia had been reported as having a cargo of chemical and biological agents aboard destined for Iraq. The ship was reported as being boarded and then, not another word.

There were reports of Scud missiles, equipped with chemical and biological payloads, being re-positioned in Iraq. John didn't quite know what to think about this information. On one hand, it was unfathomable to think anyone would release this kind of weapon. On the other hand, the good news was there was NO reporting of nuclear arms being moved or amassed in the region. A mixed blessing indeed . . .

John and the crew flew into Jedah on the West Coast of Saudi Arabia to drop off the Air Group Commander for a conference. It was there that John learned more about the jeep in Kuwait.

Sumitra Jafar was a long time contact for John. They had met more than ten years earlier in Jordan. Sumitra was glad to see John but her expression was one of concern. "I was sorry to hear about your wife, John. I know how much she meant to you."

"Thank you, Sumitra. It still seems like yesterday. Hard to believe it has been almost a year."

"No, not that. I mean about her disappearing last week."

"Last week.? I haven't seen or heard from her for almost a year. Have you heard something.?"

"I just assumed you already knew. The two Americans who are missing from that jeep in Kuwait are your wife and an agent with the Anti-Terrorist Force. The local news media seems to think they were taken hostage, but rumor has it they defected. My contact in Kuwait said they were seen leaving the city in an Iraqi truck. She was driving and there were only two of them in the vehicle. Doesn't sound like a hostage situation to me."

"I wonder what she was doing in Kuwait in the first place. It's not exactly Club Med."

"Apparently, she had been there for nearly a year. She was staying with one of the oil barons who was a long time friend of her father. I'm sorry, I thought you knew."

Suddenly many things were becoming clear. Amal Dey was an old school friend of Kate's father and his son David had been Kate's college sweetheart. Could it be Kate had opted for the life of a princess with David instead of life in suburbia with John.? Though John knew the answer, it would still take months for the reality to finally sink in. They were very long months.

John followed the news even more closely in the following days, hoping for additional news about Kate. Nothing. The story was never followed up on. The media had much bigger stories to tell. The US had started bombing Iraq.

Every day there were reports of bombers unloading over Iraq. Often there would be pictures of buildings being hit by "Smart" bombs. Probably the most impressive was the footage taken from a camera in the nose of one of the Smart bombs. The entire world got a bird's eye view. We could see the cross hairs on the target building. We could sense speed as the missile approached its mark. The footage took us right through an open window to the point of impact. The state of modern technology was truly amazing.

Of course, some of the news was met with severe criticism. Such was a particular news report from Baghdad. John and the crew were watching CNN one evening when the Stateside commentator was asking questions of their correspondent in Baghdad.

Commentator: "Can you assess the feelings of the people of Baghdad.?"

Correspondent: "Actually, I have not been allowed out of the hotel for over a week, but the people inside the hotel seem weary from all the bombing. Nobody wants to venture outside and most are getting a pretty strong dose of cabin fever."

Commentator: "Have you seen Sadam.? If so, how is he holding up.?"

Correspondent: "I saw him last evening and earlier today. He seems in good health and good spirits. He was in the company of his guard who escort him everywhere. They seem to be getting a bit behagered but, all in all, seem to be holding it together."

This news report was the start of an entire evening's debate. First of all, the news had been reporting Sadam as being held up in a 'hardened' facility beneath a hotel or hospital. Second, they reported that intelligence had been unable to pinpoint Sadam's position.

The crew went wild with their flogging of the news media. If the correspondent had seen Sadam last evening and again this morning with his escort . . . and the correspondent hadn't been outside the hotel for a week . . . and Sadam was in a 'hard' site beneath a hotel or hospital . . .

How hard was it to put those three pieces together.? The question was . . . how stupid did the news media think the public was.? The follow-up question was . . . why weren't we doing anything about what was obvious.?

Of course, every opinion was different. One person thought Sadam should be "taken out". Another agreed, but thought we should wait for his personal Guard to do it for us. Someone thought we should send one of the smart bombs into the basement of the hotel, another thought it would be political suicide because the public would see an American correspondent literally blown up, up close and personal on national TV, right there in living Technicolor. Not a pretty thought.

John thought Sadam should be taken out of power before any more harm came to the innocent people of Iraq. To John, the culprit was Sadam himself and not the people of Iraq. Civilized cultures can't have bullies putting entire countries into extinction. At the same time, they can't control a bully unless they can get to him. And there was the political risk of taking him out and losing all political influence with other countries in the region by making him a martyr. The simplest and safest course seemed to be to let things simmer for a while and hope the Elite Guard would do the job that needed to be done. If his own people took him out, the war would stop, the people of Kuwait would be safe, and the region could return to a place of stability. It also would mean the US and her allies wouldn't be seen as the aggressors. Important considerations if we were out to maintain any kind of influence in the region. John was happy NOT to be in Washington these days.

Escort Duty

The following few weeks were relatively uneventful for John and the crew. Regular hops from the ship to Saudi and Oman were punctuated with occasional trips to Diego Garcia and even an excursion back to the Philippines via Bangkok, Thailand when the Admiral had to attend briefings.

The Iraqis were back across the boarder and out of Kuwait. The Saudi were feeling more comfortable that they weren't next on Sadam's invasion list. President Bush had just called for a cessation of bombing. The military commanders were livid that they weren't allowed to "finish the job" but it looked like things were going to calm down for a while.

It was a Wednesday morning when John was summoned to the Captain's quarters. "Come in John. It's good to see you."

"It's good to see you too, sir. What can I do for you, sir.?"

"How would you and your crew like to go back to the States.?"

"Somehow, I don't think there would be any arguments from my crew, but our tour isn't up yet, sir."

"I know John, but I need someone to escort a body back

home. He was a civilian oil consultant and a retired Navy
Officer. He was killed in an explosion on one of the oil wells.
Civilian aircraft still aren't allowed in the region so we are
going to use his retired status to justify putting him on a
military airlift home. It should give you a chance to get the
rest of the information Charlie wants and deliver it to him
while it's still news. What do you say.?"

"Far be it from me to look a gift horse in the mouth.
Thank you, sir. We accept."

"Great. Why don't you go tell your crew. You can leave
first thing in the morning. It's been great having you here."

"It's been great working with you too, sir. And thanks for
making the tour interesting."

The entire crew arrived early for their morning briefing.
It had been over a year since any of them had been home.
Today was what the majority of military members looked for-
ward to most. The day they headed back home.

It was a short hop from the boat to Kuwait City. Landing
was a bit touchy since there were still holes in the runway
from the Iraqis trying to destroy the field before they left.
The city was still in shambles. Once a showcase, there were
now bullet holes in most of the buildings and bomb rubble
lining the streets. It would take years to repair all of the damage.

John went directly to the morgue when they arrived. The
plan was to make final arrangements today so they could
leave for home first thing in the morning. This would give
John some time to gather an assessment for Charlie and maybe
even enough time to close some personal loose ends. It was
going to be a busy day.

It was late morning when John arrived at the morgue to
meet with the Coroner.

John disliked meeting with coroners, morticians and
other people that work with the dead. They had always seemed
so callous, and the whole idea of being around dead people

just gave John the creeps. John had known Omar for years. He seemed sociable enough on the surface but that calm demeanor was pretty hard to cover up.

"Hello Omar," John said. "Have I caught you at a bad time.?"

"I was just heading to the hospital for a few minutes. Why don't you join me.?"

John walked with Omar for the six blocks to the hospital and got an earful.

Omar recounted the past few weeks to John's shock. Sure John had been in the thick of it many times before. People getting shot or otherwise hurt was just part of the price of war. This was different.

John learned of atrocity after atrocity committed by the Iraqi soldiers. Some of the stories were so outrageous that John started taking them all with a huge grain of salt. This guy had been doing his job too long. Omar saw the look of disbelief in John's face and invited John to accompany him to an autopsy that afternoon. John wasn't prepared for what he was about to see.

John joined Omar shortly after he had started the procedure. He could see that the deceased was a young girl. Omar spoke into the microphone in a steady, cold, quiet monotone. "Deceased is female, approximately ten years of age. She is four foot five inches tall, eighty-seven pounds, black hair, with brown eyes. Deceased's right arm has been severed just below the elbow. There are no other apparent bullet or knife wounds."

As the coroner's monologue continued, John found himself tuning it out. "Why had he been asked to observe this autopsy.?" he asked himself. This was a young girl that had apparently gotten caught in the crossfire of war. A tragedy to be sure. But why was he here.? Then John got the shock of his life.

As Omar removed the sheet that had been covering the

girl's lower body, John realized that the girl's missing arm wasn't missing at all. It had been inserted into her by whoever had committed this . . . yes . . . atrocity.

Omar told John that the girl had attempted to stay alive by allowing certain "favors" for her captors. When faced with being driven out of the city, her captors had made sure she couldn't talk and at the same time sent a message to others who may also have tales to tell.

John found himself physically ill from the sight of the young girl. This was what he had been ordered to find out. Were the stories true.? Had there been misconduct.? What was the magnitude of the situation.? What were the implications.?

John now had his answer. It would be a long flight back to the States. He was escorting one of the lucky ones. This man had been caught in an explosion in the early days of the occupation. John now knew it could have been much worse.

Kate

John Llewellyn

Dear John

John and Omar spent the rest of the morning talking about what had happened during the occupation. By the time they were finished John was simply numb. He could hardly believe what he had been hearing. If John hadn't seen some of the morgue residents himself, he still wouldn't have believed it.

John had had enough. He had the information he was sent to retrieve. Now it was time to put it aside and move on. So he thought. Omar had one more piece for John to absorb.

"There is just one more matter John. I don't know how to break this to you, so I think it is best to just get it out of the way." With this, Omar handed John an envelope simply marked, "John Llewellyn".

John recognized the handwriting. It was a letter from Kate.

"Amal asked me to give this to you when he heard you would be escorting our friend. I'm sorry I have to be the messenger, but better me than a total stranger."

John thanked Omar for his hospitality and returned to

his aircraft where he could have some privacy. It looked like it was going to be an even longer afternoon.

John and his crew finished loading their aircraft, making sure the casket was secure and that they collected all of the out-going mailbags. The trip was to be a fairly easy one. The first leg was from Kuwait to Oman, just a couple of hours of flight time, a daylight landing, and a quick refueling.

Oman was a little out of the way, but their next stop would be an overnight in Bangkok where direct flights from Iraq or Kuwait were not allowed. The stop in Oman allowed the crew to refuel and pick up mail from the US Postmaster which could have easily taken another month to get back to the States, while changing their departure point from Kuwait to Oman.

Bangkok stopovers were usually planned as early morning arrivals and departures. This practice let the flight crews have a day to shop and see the sights, and still get a good night's sleep before their morning departure. And, of course, there was the added bonus of getting a Thailand stamp in your passport.

John found himself thankful for the short overnight stopover, but didn't expect to get much sleep. He still couldn't bring himself to open Kate's letter.

Morning came much too soon. Preflight was at eight, so the crew had to be out of their hotel by seven. John had already been awake for over an hour when his alarm went off.

Flight preparations went smoothly and they were in the air headed for the Philippines by 0930. It was a comfortable and easy flight for everyone, except for John whose mind was still on Kate's unopened letter . . .

The weather in the Philippines was, somewhat appropriately, low cloud cover and heavy drizzle for their arrival. After making sure the aircraft and crew were all taken care of, John climbed back into the front seat of the aircraft and prepared himself for the worst. As he opened the envelope, John found that he wasn't far off . . .

Dear John,

I'm sorry to have to write this letter (and I truly regret the salutation), but I feel it is for the best. As you know, my father and Amal have been best friends for decades. When you received orders to remain on active Navy duty, I simply couldn't take it. I needed time and space to sort through my life and figure out what was really important to me in it.

I left Washington and came to stay with Amal in Kuwait. Little did I know what was to happen while I was here. I know now why you had to leave, and how hard it was for you. I have never met a more loving and caring person. I am sorry that your love was wasted on me.

Living here in Kuwait has reminded me of what it is like to bask in the lap of luxury. I missed the pampering and lack of responsibility that comes with material wealth. I guess I'm just too much of a material girl to settle for the American dream.

I spoke with Father a few months back and he has arranged for our divorce. The final papers will be waiting for you with Charlie when you return home. All you need to do is sign them and everything will be completed. I'm sorry to do things this way, but I just couldn't face seeing you again.

I have left this letter with Amal so he may find a way to get it to you before you go back to the States. As you may have guessed, I am no longer in Kuwait but well on my way to South America. Please believe I have given this a great deal of thought. This is the only way. I'm sure there is someone out there who will be

*much more receptive to your total love and commit-
ment than me.*

*I know you have been totally loyal and faithful
even in light of my disappearance and lack of contact
for the last year. I appreciate your feelings and loyalty,
but it is time for you to let go and get on with your life.*

I love you very much.

Kate

Home from the sea

It was a morning of mixed feelings when John and the crew boarded the Air Force transport headed for Hawaii and the first leg of their return trip home. It was a relief to know they were headed home and nice to let someone else be responsible to fly the plane and take care of them for a change.

On the other hand, they would probably never fly together again as a crew. This crew had been together for nearly a year and a half. They had become like family to each other, sharing the day's highs and lows, successes and failures, not to mention the unmentionables of a bunch of men sharing the inside of an airplane not much larger than a typical bathroom for all that time. It was like saying goodbye to your brothers or children who were leaving home.

The crew stayed together until they arrived in Hawaii. From there John was put on a connecting flight with his 'cargo', and the rest of the crew boarded a contracted 747 for their next leg on the journey home.

It was a long flight back to the mainland for John. The day was full of reflection, smiles and an occasional tear. It was the beginning of spring when John arrived in Washington. The snows had melted and the flowers had started to bloom.

As John stood waiting for his luggage at Baggage Claim he noticed a man holding up a sign . . .

"Llewellyn"

"I am John Llewellyn." he said to the man.

"Welcome home, Mr. Llewellyn. I have a car outside. May I help you with your luggage.?"

John was pleased with the reception. Arriving home always summoned up memories of arriving home from Viet Nam. It was a "non" event. Nobody was at the airport to meet him when he arrived at LA International. There were no crowds, no bands and no ceremonies. In fact, the only recurring memory was of the person who spat upon him and spewed obscenities as he deplaned at the terminal.

This return was quite different. In Hawaii, San Francisco and in Washington there was someone to meet him. Nothing spectacular, just a handshake, smile and a simple "Welcome Home". Like most veterans, John didn't think it was a lot to ask in return for risking his life for his country.

For the next week there were debriefings, "official" dinners and lunches with politicians & friends. Between Charlie and Georgia, John was kept busy almost non-stop.

Georgia, breaking from her long-standing norms, had John and several of his friends over to dinner and the most scrumptious strawberry tort for desert. Part way through the evening, Georgia announced that this was a "dual" celebration. Not only was she celebrating John's return and retirement, but hers as well.

It was all set. Georgia had arranged to retire on the same day as John. Charlie, feeling a bit deserted I'm sure, had also decided to close this chapter of his life and was planning to retire at the end of his tour in November.

It was all coming to a close. Everyone was back safely, except Keith who was returning in the morning, and all were gathered to bid a fond farewell. The celebration was started and all knew it would shift into high gear as soon as Keith arrived . . .

There were only two more days. The celebrations, parties, debriefings and obligatory politicking would be over and John could return home. Home to new projects, new opportunities and most of all, a newfound control over his time and life. No flight schedules, briefings or 2 a.m. rescue flights. Just sunrise, sunset, a small farm to attend to, and of course, a roadster to build.

==

Friday was a long day for John. The day had been choreographed down to the smallest detail. Up at 7 a.m., an hour in the gym and a good shower to get the day started off right. These would be followed by last minute packing, checking out of Officers' Quarters and getting his bags on their way to the airport.

John's retirement was at 9 a.m. and Georgia's at 10:45. They had tried for a combined session but red tape prevailed. Somehow, a Navy Officer and a Civil Service employee weren't allowed to "fraternize" to the point of combining their ceremonies. They had discussed "retiring together separately" by both retiring at 10 a.m. but decided it would be quite fitting to let the government have it's way, just one more time, and roll with this last minute "inconvenience".

After the formal retirement, Charlie, Georgia and John would have a quiet catered lunch in Charlie's private office and John would leave for the airport by 2 p.m. to make his flight to Chicago.

In Chicago John was meeting with a man who had just finished restoring an old Victoria Coupe and was preparing to build a new roadster from the ground up. John had been corresponding with Mark for nearly six months. This was an

opportune time to meet him face-to-face before starting a
roadster of his own. As it turned out, they were both huge
baseball fans and had arranged to meet at Wrigley Field for
the night game. Second row, right next to first base. It just
didn't get any better than that . . .

From Chicago it would be the red-eye to Denver, pick up
a rental car and drive down to Colorado Springs . . .

Home Again

It was wonderful to be back home again in Colorado. The hills were green, the air fresh and even the birds were happy as they fluttered across the cool morning sky. There weren't many cars on the road this morning, too early probably.

As John neared Colorado Springs he began recognizing more and more of the landscape. So much had changed, and yet so much was exactly as he had left it.

Most of the fields had been plowed in preparation for the spring planting. There were tractors in the fields awaiting their farmers who would move from field to field. Everyone had his or her part this time of year. Some drove tractors grooming the fields, others would walk the rows planting seed. Another group would be moving irrigation pipe while others would be preparing food for the noon meal.

It was only about another mile before John would get to his childhood home. There would be much to do. The house had been leased for several years before getting boarded up nearly five years ago. John would need to remove the plywood from the windows and doors that had been protection from the elements. There would be lots of cleaning, painting and probably much of the furniture would have to be replaced. It would be a lot of work but John was looking forward to reuniting with his roots.

As John approached the farm he could see Keith's father in the north field and pulled to the side of the road. It was wonderful to see Mr. Johnson looking so happy and . . . familiar. He looked exactly as he had over twenty years ago. The wrinkles had gotten a bit deeper around the edges of his eyes when he smiled, and his sideburns were now almost completely white, but the warmth of his presence was unmistakably the same. Yes, John was finally home.

"Have you been to the house yet John.?"

"Not yet. I was on the first flight into Denver this morning. Have you heard from Keith.?"

"Keith called last night. He's still debriefing in Washington but said he expects to be home in a couple weeks."

"Some of our friends helped open the house last week-end. The electricity is on but it's gonna' take a while for the water to clear up since the well hasn't been used for so many years. We had a steer break a leg and had to put him down so Mr. Pratz, the butcher, has a hind quarter waiting for you as soon as your freezer gets cold."

"Thank you. It means a lot to be received with such a warm welcome."

"It's the least we can do, John. Besides, we want to see you get off to a good start."

"I very much appreciate it. Guess I'd better get on over there and start getting settled."

"See you in a few days John."

"What an odd thing to say," John thought to himself. "I wonder if he's going out of town for a few days. Hmmm . . . "

Home was just around the corner, a path John had taken hundreds of times before. As he drove down the lane to his home, he noticed a chord of wood out by the woodshed and then a whisp of smoke coming from the chimney.

There was a light on over the porch and as John walked up to the house, the front door opened.

"Care for your slippers sailor.?"

Johns knees went soft and he nearly stumbled as he recognized the statuesque figure in the doorway. "Kym.! What are you doing here.?"

"Where else in the world would I be, other than by the side of the man I love.?"

"But I thought . . . "

"No you didn't. I've been yours since Guam. There is no other man for me, never has been, and never will be. The only question is . . . How do YOU feel.?"

"I've always loved you. I didn't think you would ever consider me in that light. I'm quite a bit older than . . ."

"Stop.! That's enough. John, I chose you. I want to spend the rest of my life with you, bearing your children and enjoying each and every one of the days to come with you. If you'll have me."

"Of course I'll have you. I never in my wildest dreams thought you wanted me.! You have made me the happiest man on earth."

"Not yet. Why don't you come inside, and we'll see what we can do . . . "

. . . Guess Mr. Johnson was right . . . He wouldn't see John for a few days . . . . ;-)

For your further consideration

As with any good story there is always the 'untold'. *Allies of the Storm* was originally started in 1992 to offer another perspective to the possibilities of the flow of events surrounding Desert Shield and Desert Storm.

It was once said that those who refuse to learn from the events of history are doomed to repeat them. Is the world again going down that much traveled path.?

There are many examples of super powers being brought down by the small and meek. David brought down Goliath, not with overwhelming power, but with a simple slingshot. Oh, but that was just a fairytale . . .

In Viet Nam, when facing formidable and relentless opponents, chaos was caused when grenades were strapped to little children, exploding when they were greeted by trusting American soldiers who let their guards down. Imagine feeling reluctant, or even fearful, of reaching out to nurture and comfort a crying child. This tears at the very fabric of humanity.

In Oklahoma it was a rented truck, not filled with nuclear material, but with fertilizer. In Yemen it was a little boat helping a US Navy ship tie up to the dock, that exploded and took over a dozen lives and seriously injured several dozen more. Let us not forget the Marine barracks, the Trade Towers, the airliners and . . . well, you know the list as well as I.

Whether it be for religious conviction, the feeling of power or a simple act of insanity, the fact still remains . . . No matter how big, no matter how powerful, no matter how technologically advanced, no matter how well adapted, . . . nothing is totally invincible. Anyone who doesn't realize this might want to reflect, for a moment, about the fate of the dinosaur . . . probably put into extinction by the common cold.

H.G.Wells even brought a country to a standstill as an audience became caught up in a radio broadcast of his *War of the Worlds*. Let us not forget that this overwhelming destructive power, on which even the best weaponry had no effect, was rendered helpless by a common virus.

Again, and again, we encounter this repeating theme. Hollywood even got into the act with its blockbuster *Independence Day*. And let us not forget Master Luke and his rag-tag attack on the invincible Battle Star.

Some of these events transformed us as they faded from today's news to yesterday's history. Others simply fueled our imaginations until we re-grounded ourselves in the realities of our lives.

As news becomes history, and imagination slips away into subliminal inspiration, we settle into the security we feel in the knowledge that we are invincible, until we return to reality. Sometimes it's an accident, other times deliberate reflection, that brings us home again.

Hopefully *Allies of the Storm* has touched a thread of your reality. Whether it was romance lost or romance found, the comfort of John coming home safely, or the picture of a young girl in the morgue, hopefully something hit home. I, for one, sleep better at night knowing that there are those, like Keith and John, who go the extra yard to help us feel safe and secure.

Following are a couple of possible timelines. Take your pick, or generate your own. After all, it's your future too . . .

View One—
The Optimist...

- General—Mr. President, intelligence has determined that Sadam is on the verge of being able to deliver both nuclear and biological threats within the next six months. In our opinion it is imperative that we neutralize this threat in the near term.
- President—Have you a plan General ?
- General—Yes sir. The joint chiefs and our military brain trust have come up with the following scenario. Normal Fleet rotation is coming up in late July. We could pull the carrier task group out of the Indian Ocean, replenish their supplies and augment their weapons stores in that time frame to avoid drawing attention to the buildup. The relieving task group could be provisioned with the augments as they pass Hawaii to avoid drawing the attention they would get if we were to do it in the Philippines. We could have

TWO, fully provisioned, carrier groups on station in the Gulf of Oman by mid August without drawing significant attention. This would create a lack of coverage in the area for the first two weeks of August, but we believe having two fully armed carrier groups in the area is essential if we are to manage a swift and complete destruction of Iraq's arsenal and their mechanism to rebuild.

- President—In that case . . . Make it so. . . . And let's keep it quiet . . .

Aug 2, 1990: **Iraq invades Kuwait**.

- President—Where do we stand.?

- General–Iraq has made a full force invasion into Kuwait. Our carrier groups are still in the Philippines and are getting underway. The new carrier group should depart within 24 hours and the other should be 48 hours behind them to allow us time to complete their provisioning.

- Intel–Sir, this could actually be a blessing in disguise. With Iraq attacking Kuwait, we are likely to be looked at as the rescuer instead of the aggressor.

- President–If Sadam keeps cooperating like this, we could all still have jobs next year.

Jan 31 , 1991: **Oval Office**

- President—I think we are doing pretty well. Where do we stand.?

- General—Overall, we have managed to get most of the nuclear and biological storage facilities. We believe we have managed to get ALL of his production facilities.

- President–Very well, I think it is time to wind this down before we wear out our welcome.

Feb , 1991: **Gulf war ends**

Jan , 1992: **Iraq fights back**

- Sadam–We need to recover from this setback. How can we keep the Americans occupied while we recover and establish a new plan.?
- Guard–We should stall as much as possible. We could leak information to the press that there are weapons in the desert and hills. When they want to inspect, we could stall and block them from getting access.
- Sadam–Very good. Hold them off until they threaten to invade us, then let the infidels inspect at the last minute. Of course, they wouldn't find anything, and we use that as evidence to the Americans oppression and attempts to bully us.
- Guard–All of our neighbors would be threatened by the Americans aggressions, and forget about Kuwait. Brilliant.!

Nov , 1998: **Iraq blocks international inspectors**

- US and Allies use the opportunity to start bombing Iraqi locations which are suspected of housing the storage and manufacturing facilities of chemical, biological and nuclear weapons.
- Intelligence uncovers information that there are NO weapons or manufacturing facilities left in Iraq. Fortunately, the information reaches the US president in time to recall the first wave of heavy bombers before they unloaded on Iraq, saving the US from making Sadam a martyr.
- The Arab nations unite in forcing Iraq to open all facilities to international inspectors.
- Inspections reveal NO weapons, or means to manufacture weapons, anywhere in Iraq.
- The people of Iraq revolt, removing Sadam from power and forcing him into exile in Bogota. The Colombian drug cartel puts an end to Sadam when they mistake his construction of a manufacturing plant and chemical lab as competition to their drug machine.

Jan 1, 2000 :—Palestinian and Israeli reach millennium peace accord, deciding to share the holy ground.

■   The world is stunned when headlines around the world read . . .

" Millennium Begins In Peace"

View TWO – Allies . . .

Feb 1, 1990: **Washington DC—Oval Office**

- General—Mr. President, intelligence has determined that Sadam is on the verge of being able to deliver both nuclear and biological threats within the next six months. In our opinion it is imperative that we neutralize this threat in the near term.
- President—Have you a plan General?
- General—Yes sir. The joint chiefs and our military brain trust have come up with the following scenario. As we all know Sadam has been itching to get into Kuwait in order to exploit the oil fields to fund the buildup of his Army. Why don't we give him a window of opportunity.? We could "inadvertently" have a lapse of US Military presence in the gulf region. Sadam wouldn't be able to resist the temptation. Once Sadam has taken the bait and entered Kuwait we would be able to "retaliate" and eliminate their nuclear/biological production facilities in the process. Political projections predict considerable worldwide support for "rescuing" Kuwait and minimal opposition.

Besides, many of our 750-pound bombs are approaching the end of their shelf life. This could be an opportunity to freshen our stockpile with little or no opposition from Congress.

- President—Sounds reasonable. Do you have a proposed time frame.?

- General—Yes sir. Late July to Early August in conjunction with normal fleet rotation. This would raise the least suspicion.

- President—In that case . . . Make it so. . . . And let's keep it quiet . . .

Aug 2, 1990: **Iraq invades Kuwait**.

Feb , 1991: **Gulf war ends—Oval Office**

- President—I think that went pretty well. Where do we stand.?

- General—Overall, we managed to get most of the nuclear and biological production facilities. There have been reports that Sadam managed to remove much of the inventory before the production facilities were destroyed. He may not be able to produce any more for a while but we would all feel a bit easier if we knew where his stockpile was being stored.

Thanksgiving 1994: **Oval office**

- FBI—Mr. President. At 0429 this morning our operatives located a thermal nuclear device in Los Angeles. The device was apparently brought into the city in small pieces and assembled in the basement of a large office building. The device was set to go off at 0800 on December 7th (Pearl Harbor Day), right in the middle of rush hour. It has been dismantled and further analysis is in progress.

- President—How large was this device.?

- FBI—The device is capable of destroying the entire Los Angeles Basin. Its location appears to have been very carefully selected. The weapons destruction would be both confined to, and concentrated by, the mountain ranges surrounding Los Angeles. This weapon could have destroyed one third of the population of California and put the rest of the country into panic.
- President—Do we know the origin if this weapon.?
- FBI—Not at this time, but we believe the only unaccounted for nuclear source of this magnitude was supposedly destroyed in Iraq during the Gulf War.
- President—Keep me appraised . . .

December 1, 1994: **Oval office**

- CIA—Mr. President. We have received a demand for the removal of all military forces outside of the continental US borders. The source states that there are nuclear and biological devices in major cities throughout the United States. We have been given one week to respond.
- President—Is it possible these threats are real.?
- CIA—Given the device found in Los Angeles, and intelligence reports that there is enough unaccounted for nuclear material from the Gulf War to construct approximately seven more devices like it . . . Yes sir, we think it is possible.
- President—Pearl Harbor all over . . . Any idea of WHY this might be happening..?
- CIA—Intelligence believes that this is an attempt to neutralize the last global peacekeeper. US.

- Even if they are not totally successful. It would render the US unable to project power beyond our own borders and force us to assume an isolationistic posture. Meanwhile, we would not have the means to interfere with radical factions abroad. With the ineffective histories of NATO and the United Nations, it basically means every country has to fend for itself instead of waiting for the US to protect them.
- President—Not a pretty picture. You've not mentioned the biological possibilities . . .
- CIA—We really have little to base our projections from. However, we have evidence to support there being enough biologic agent to affect nearly one half of the earth's surface. Again, NOT a pretty picture . . .
- President—What are the projections for probable targets within the US.?
- Intelligence–Mr. President, we expect that the first targets would be with the largest impact on the feelings of security to the entire nation as a whole.

The most obvious would be Washington, D.C. Major state population centers such as New York, Los Angeles, Seattle and San Francisco would likely be targeted next. Los Angeles and San Francisco could be a bit higher priority since they are located in valleys, which would tend to both confine and concentrate the effectiveness of an airborne agent.

All of these cities have perfect launching sites with the Trade Towers, Space Needle and TransAmerica buildings as examples.

With these five targets alone it would be hard to find anyone, anywhere else in the country who wouldn't lose a family member, business associate or loved one. The emotional impact would be devastating.

The next level would probably target industrial, technology and business centers. San Jose, San Diego, Dallas and Chicago would likely head that list.

In short, I'm especially glad I don't live, or work, on the West Coast.

Somewhere in there we would surely lose the remotes of Guam, Hawaii and Alaska since they would be the most likely rallying points for our military to try and regroup. These locations would be more likely to come under conventional assaults in light of limited biological resources and the desire to eliminate all infrastructures that could facilitate our re-mobilization at one of these locations.

Summer 1998:

- —API—Countries in the Persian Gulf region begin underground nuclear testing.

October 1998:

- Intelligence–Mr. President. We have indication Iraq has begun manufacture and storage of large quantities of bacteriological agents.
- Presidential Advisor—With the Presidency facing imminent impeachment proceedings, we feel we need to act quickly to divert public attention abroad. To this end, we recommend preparing for large-scale bombings of Iraqi centers of agent production and storage.

November 1998:

- Iraq blocks international inspectors
- US uses the opportunity to commence bombing Iraqi facilities which manufacture and/or store chemical/ biological agents.
- Settlement in key court case relating to the President & impeachment.
- A meteor shower jeopardizes surveillance satellites that monitor Iraq.
- Bombers are recalled, in mid-flight, delaying the destruction of Iraqi weapons production facilities.

December 7, 1999: **US-1 Airborne over the Atlantic**

- Intelligence–Mr. President. We have confirmed

biological releases in San Francisco, New York, Seattle, San Diego and Washington DC. There has been no communication from any of these cities since the detonations. We have received communications from Iraq claiming responsibility. We have also received communication from Iraq demanding that we recall all overseas military personnel and hardware or risk an additional series of biological detonations, one each day until the demands are met.

- President—You have authorization for submarine ballistic missile launches to eliminate the countries of Iran and Iraq.

The entire Gulf region was destabilized. Fearing the escalation, former members of the Soviet Union prepared to protect their borders. European countries saw the escalation in the communist block and raised their defenses . . .

December 21, 1999 Global nuclear and Biological war begins.

January 1, 2000 <you choose> declares sovereignty over the remaining inhabitants of . . . Earth . . .

View THREE—Yours

. . .